THE STORY COLLECTO

ARCHITECT
OF THE
MIST

E.S. BARRISON

Architect of the Mist/E.S. Barrison. -- 1st ed.
ISBN 979-8-9853634-7-0

Dedicated to Grandma Rhoda & Grandpa David

It's hard to dedicate a story about a villain to two people I loved dearly. But you taught me everyone has a story.

So I'll tell this one too.

THE COUNCIL OF MIST KEEPERS

NINGURSU
The God of Death

AELIA
The Healer

TOMAS
The Peacemaker

JULIETTA
The Painter

JIANG
Null

MALAIKA
The Cartographer

ALOJZY
The Architect

CAROLINE
The Illusionist

BRENT
The Story Collector

AL·MA·NAC

a publication containing astronomical or meteorological infor-
mation, as future positions of celestial objects, star magnitudes,
and culmination dates of constellations.

FOREWARD

Not all stories deserve a pedestal.

Some belong in a drawer or buried in a hole.

Forgotten.

But I'm not in the business of forgetting stories.

It wasn't my choice to join the Council of Mist Keepers. Rather, fate thrust it upon me when my teacher, Caroline Walsh, brought me to the Library deep in the heart of the earth. This Library harbored more stories than I ever imagined.

And soon, I would become one of their keepers.

Yet the Library itself has a story far darker than the tales of the dead. Built by an architect with an obsessive vendetta, the Library was no sanctuary. Rather, this was the home of fallacies and domination.

This was the home that the Architect built to hide.

He did not build it to protect. No, he built it to torture and rule.

I should have known when I first met the Architect, a duplicitous and manipulative man named Alojzy, that something was amiss. Alojzy wore a guise of composure, but behind that mask hid a man driven by a distorted ambition of divinity.

At first, I didn't notice. I was young and naïve, overtaken by the endless tales before me in the Library of my dreams.

Only later did I realize the darkness that place held. Unleashing a monster was an accident, a mistake...but that monster unveiled the true nature of the Library and the prisoners it harbored deep within its crypts. With their escape came the stories the Council so desperately wanted to hide.

And these stories flicker like a dim candle, begging to be extinguished.

But it is my sworn duty to continue fanning the flame.

With these candles in my hands, I bring you the fire of Alojzy's tale. I want to say I do not agree with this man. His cares have only ever been for himself and no one else. He will do what he needs to accomplish his goals, whether the cost is the lives of the innocent or their humanity.

But now that I've chosen to tell his story, it will forever be part of me.

Because I am the Story Collector.

And I will not let the truth flicker into darkness.

-Brenton Rob Harley
Ninth Member of the Council of Mist Keepers
The Story Collector

-

ONE

O n the eve of his twelfth birthday, Alojzy selected his god. His father led him out onto the
Schanifeld, the black-and-white checkered
field that extended beyond the border of Evylain, and
there, he decided.

Like all the children before him, Alojzy had waited for
this day. He had picked apart his father's books, listened
to his mother as she described their gods, and weighed
his options in each hand. Whichever god he chose would
define his life, and it was not a decision to take lightly.

He stood on the edge of the Schanifeld beside his father, flowers decorating the field and guarded by the
pine forest where he used to play. The time for fun and
games ended the moment he selected his god, so he had
to be prepared.

This was it; this would begin his life.

His father cleared his throat. "I apologize your mother cannot be here today, Alojzy. As you know, the war with Kainan continues to brew in the south."

"I understand, Father." Alojzy laced his hands behind his back. He'd grown up with the constant nagging of war on the border, and his mother's routine disappearances no longer phased him. She joined the strongest men and women, the most powerful magicians, to fight off the Kainan foe. The reason for the war? Alojzy didn't know. No one really did. But throughout his life, the warning blared: the men of Kainan did not support Evylain's gods.

To avoid succumbing to the Kainan forces, Alojzy had to select one.

His father removed a piece of paper from his pocket. He glanced over it before saying, "Today is the day, as decreed—"

Alojzy interjected, "Father, I've already memorized the decree."

"It is customary, Alojzy. You should know that by now."

Alojzy huffed but didn't argue. The sooner this ended, the sooner he could choose.

His father continued, "As decreed, on this day, the gods Leycie and Moltod ended their centuries of war to create a soul. So may it be that all of us and you–Alojzy Gorski, son of Gerick and Felcia—entered this world. But every soul enters this world on a gamble. This gamble was one indeed that Leycie and Moltod held dear: would you, Alojzy, choose the path that Leycie lay before you or the one that Moltod left instead? Would you choose a path of affirmations, of evidence, and of light? Or would you choose a path of independence, of abstract, and of night? They have waited all these years to hear your decision, holding their wagers close and their own prayers closer. Today is the day you choose that path. Truth or belief? Support or independence? White or black? The choice is yours. So be it."

Alojzy's father dropped the paper and turned to his son. His voice cracked when he murmured, "I hope you choose the right path."

Alojzy smirked at his father, bouncing on the balls of his feet. His heart pattered in his chest. As the excitement welled in his throat, he took a deep breath, pulling back his emotions before finally speaking, "Yes, Father. I have studied long and hard. I know my path."

"Very well," his father's expression straightened. "I shall turn my back. Your choice of god is yours alone to make. It is not my place to influence your decision."

Alojzy didn't move until his father turned away from him. While the choice of god was a private manner, families usually shared their decisions. His parents both had followed Leycie since their twelfth birthdays, and while this decision was his alone to make, his parents had pressured him silently his entire life to follow the path of Leycie. They would leave books out about the god, which Alojzy devoured with curiosity. They would whisper Leycie's prayer over dinner. Even at night, through the thin walls, Alojzy heard talk of their god.

He had to admit, a god that built a kingdom from absolutes held its appeal. Why wonder when the truth was right in front of you?

Why not fall into a deep support network?

Why not stay in the light?

But ever since Alojzy had been a child, the night called to him. He would sneak out into the streets just to count the stars. When his parents weren't around, he would borrow books about Moltod and read beneath his waning candlelight. Moltod made no promises; in Moltod's world, everything existed as a mere abstract. Nothing was definite.

And Alojzy could build whatever world he wanted. He could escape the routine, redefine the definitive, and build his own castle.

He'd known in his heart which god he would choose long before his twelfth birthday.

Confidence welling in his chest, he marched onto the Schanifeld. The white and black flowers stroked at his ankles, beckoning him to either side. But he ignored their pulls, walking straight to the first fully black square and planting his feet in its center. He waited, letting the night air wrap around him.

Part of him expected something grand, but Moltod had never been the type of god for resplendent gestures. Rather, a deep chill arched over his skin.

It had to be Moltod whispering, "I'm here."

Alojzy took a knee, smiling to himself, then whispered, "And I shall stay. So be it."

The chill departed. One at a time, with the delicacy of a threading a needle, Alojzy removed one of the black-petaled flowers from the ground. He cupped it in his hands, brought it to his nose to sniff, then crumpled it in his palms.

For a moment, beneath the moonlight, a dark smudge crossed his palms like blood.

Then it vanished like smoke, securing him in the grasp of Moltod.

TWO

Alojzy wore his god close to his chest. Whenever his parents mentioned Leycie, he merely smiled, often complimenting their god's prowess but never giving away his loyalty. It was a private matter. Even if his parents would continue their love for him, he knew that if they found out he followed Moltod, disappointment would follow their every step.

He said his prayers in private, bowed his head in subservience, and gathered the pieces of his future with precision. With Moltod as his guide, a voice of question and abstract, he navigated the pathway to his future.

He buried himself in books, reading about the castles and fortresses built in Moltod's name. In the dark of night, with a single candle burning, he would sketch out his own stronghold. Beside each image, he detailed a personal crest: the headless body of Moltod sitting upon a throne, letting the world change while his rule remained.

Alojzy did not let his imagination exist only on paper. Most days, he ventured into the forest. There, he built a private altar that mimicked his dream, where he would pray to Moltod without his parent's knowledge. In the forest, by Moltod's hand, he learned.

He dove into the prayers, but he also observed. In the shadows, he lurked as young lovers met outside of wedlock, as soldiers trained without supervision, and as the men of Kainan built campsites on the Schanifeld.

The Schanifeld existed as the battlefield between Evylain and Kainan, with the town of Freiborn serving as its guard. Alojzy's parents warned him of those men; they called them slurs and profanities, halfhearted worshippers of the gods. But curiosity always struck Alojzy.

After constructing his miniature altar each day, he'd ventured to the edge of the forest to watch the Kainan soldiers as they left their battles with the fighters from Evylain. At first, he kept his distance, but as he spied on them, he became in tune with their humanity. These men of Kainan prayed to Moltod like he did, built their altars each night, and sang songs around the fire.

His fear of the men from Kainan deteriorated, and each day, he moved slightly closer to the campsite. Finally, he could hear them from his hiding spot. They spoke the same Ainan language as his own people, though their accent was slightly thicker, as if food always filled their mouths. Laughter bellowed as they gathered, roasting rabbits over the fire and throwing jugs of bier in the air.

Alojzy kept his distance.

Moltod preached patience. With patience, he could create; with patience, he had an eternity.

So Alojzy listened to their prayers.

And one day, a certain prayer struck him. A Kainan Kapitän preached by the fire just within Alojzy's earshot. He said, "And so Moltod departed, patiently waiting for the day of Leycie's surrender, with his angels on his heels. For one day, Leycie, she will submit. She will be his again. For everything returns to Moltod."

"But Leycie is powerful," a subordinate argued. "She will overcome us."

"What you are saying is propaganda from Evylain. That Leycie and Moltod are equal is repulsive. Leycie is not powerful; she is a temporary force that will always submit to the eternity that is Moltod's realm."

"You talk of Leycie like she is a woman. But she is a god. She is powerful. She won't just submit to us."

The Kapitän smacked the younger man across the face.

Alojzy winced at the sound.

The Kapitän then snarled and spat, "It is those like you who make Moltod weak. Put your faith in our god, for he guides us through this war."

"An endless war," the younger man grumbled.

"Because you lack faith. Evylain survives because they believe Moltod and Leycie are equals. The moment they learn Leycie is no god, our war may end. Instead, they choose to divide their people, allow them to choose their faith. Half of them believe Leycie brings peace, but her inability to be daring only creates chaos. It leads to the misuse of magic, to the creation of monsters, and to the abandonment of sense." The Kapitän paced around his subordinate. "Which you, Herr Pavlov, seem to have forgotten."

"I only ask questions."

"Perhaps you ask questions because you, too, want to follow Leycie."

"No. I am loyal to Moltod and Kainan."

"Then prove it."

The Kapitän handed Herr Pavlov a knife. Herr Pavlov stared at it for a moment, then lifted the knife and stabbed himself in the leg. The man winced but didn't move, letting the blood drip from his leg.

The Kapitän nodded and took the knife back. "That'll do, Herr Pavlov. Thank you."

Alojzy watched as the men continued their meal as if nothing had happened. They knew so much about Moltod; were the books in Evylain hiding the truth? Did Moltod really deserve to be worshipped by everyone?

Perhaps. He chose Moltod, after all.

Alojzy didn't want to risk being seen by these men. As they returned to their meal, he slinked back into the forest. His altar waited for him, as always. Designed to look like a castle with a sketch of Moltod's headless body staring straight at him, it beckoned him, demanding he show his loyalty.

Alojzy paused, then raised his hand and scraped it against the bark of a nearby tree. Blood gathered in the center of his palm.

He held his hand over the altar and squeezed it tight.

Three drops of blood fell, landing on the sketched crest of Moltod himself, like a quiet prayer.

THREE

Alojzy couldn't keep his beliefs hidden from his family forever. His constant disappearance into the forest came with questions, and occasionally, he even found the words of the men from Kainan on his lips. He admired their determination and power, their utmost respect for Moltod. After all, Moltod survived even in darkness; Leycie relied solely on the unfounded belief of her worshippers.

But he couldn't say that to his parents.

If they found out he had been listening to the Kainan warriors, what might they do? His mother was a member of the Evylain Army; she certainly wouldn't let him continue his treason.

Alojzy concocted an array of possibilities each day, building each one out of the ashes of the next. His mother could send him to jail. They might brainwash him into believing in Leycie, or perhaps it might even mean death. At his altar each day, he asked Moltod for clarity. Alojzy understood better than anyone that Moltod would continue to mull in the abstract as if locked deep in a fog of night and death. Moltod did not decide the path of life. Rather, Moltod let the world thrive in chaos, then collected the souls from the ashes to build his kingdom.

For those who followed Leycie, the thought was hard to fathom. But Alojzy recognized the truth: Moltod was the master of death.

He almost let it slip one day over dinner with his parents, but to his relief, they didn't say a word.

At least not until soon after his fifteenth birthday.

One day, upon leaving the forest after another day of spying on the men from Kainan and praying to his altar, he found his father walking home from the small fortress owned by the notorious Goryl Family. A resplendent structure that towered above the rest of the town of Freiborn, the Goryl family marked the town with prosperity. All because three hundred years earlier, the Dame Boguslawa Goryl led the fight against the men of Kainan in a battle. Her army fought back for weeks, and ultimately, the men of Kainan retreated, never to infiltrate the northern city again. Even now, the Kainan opposition avoided Freiborn, and the Goryl Family maintained a place of honor in the city even after all these years, with their matriarchs holding the gavel of war.

Alojzy slowed upon seeing his father leaving the Goryl home. His father caught sight of him at once. "Ah, Alojzy, my son. Where were you?"

"The forest, as usual, Father." Alojzy eyed his father closely. "More importantly, what are you doing here?"

His father laughed. "I am sure you know that I have been repairing Herr Sauer and Dame Goryl's shoes for many years now."

"Yes, but never in their home. They send their servants."

His father laughed again. "Well—"

"Father, please do not lie to me." Alojzy crossed his arms. *This is what you get for following Leycie, Father. You think people will have your back and pass you affirmations. That is not the way the world works.*

At first, his father didn't reply, merely rubbing his hands together and glancing back at the Goryl estate. "Dame Goryl has much respect for the work your mother and I do. Your mother fights alongside the Dame, and I have been mending their shoes for many years. It has allowed us to build a friendship. And, well, she...has a proposition."

Alojzy waited for his father to elaborate.

"You are fifteen, my son. You'll be a man soon...and you'll need to choose a partner in this life." His father licked his bottom lip, then continued, "Dame Goryl has five daughters. Her youngest daughter, Dobroslawa, is a miraculous fighter, but she is not in line to inherit their home."

"What does this have to do with me, Father?"

"Alojzy, you have an eye for architecture. I have seen your sketches."

Alojzy froze. If his father discovered his sketches, then that had to mean one thing.

His father answered his worries with a single statement: "Your fortress to the god Moltod is quite remarkable."

"So you know who I chose?" Alojzy mumbled.

"I always knew." His father smiled. "I am glad you chose the path of your heart."

Alojzy scowled. He expected his father to yell. Yet his parents, as pure devotees of Leycie, never looked for an altercation. If his father were to argue, perhaps Alojzy could convince him why Moltod was better. But they didn't argue; they didn't fight. It left Alojzy feeling useless against them.

Would they yell at him if they knew he watched the men of Kainan? He almost considered telling his father but honed in on his current battle instead. For now, he wouldn't argue with them either.

"I apologize for invading your privacy, my son," his father said. "A few weeks back, Herr Sauer came to pick up his shoes...which shocked me to no end! In a fit of nerves, I ran upstairs to get his new pair of shoes, and that's when I saw your door was ajar. The window was open. A gust of wind picked one of your drawings off your desk, and I raced to catch it. Herr Sauer heard the commotion and came to help...and that's when we discovered your architectural sketches." His father once again wrung his hands together, then said, "We didn't mean to look, of course, but we could help but notice. I didn't realize Herr Sauer had pocketed one of your sketches."

Alojzy furrowed his brow. He had lost track of many of his sketches. No wonder he didn't notice.

His father continued, "A few days later, Dame Goryl summoned me. She saw your sketches and admires your talent, Alojzy."

"Father, I would appreciate it if you could be direct with me. Please." Alojzy clenched his jaw, swallowing back his frustration.

"Yes, of course." His father chuckled slightly, then said, "Dame Goryl is offering to finance your endeavor to build a Citadel to Moltod on the edge of the

Schanifeld. She believes it will show balance to the Castle of Leycie in the city center."

The tension in Alojzy's shoulders released. He never thought that someone would help him achieve his goal. Nor did he ever expect his father to facilitate it.

But everything had a cost.

"What is the caveat?" Alojzy asked.

"In exchange, you will marry the young Dobroslawa Goryl in five years when she returns from her training. The Citadel you build will be more than just a prayer to your god but a home for both of you."

Alojzy squinted at his father, then out towards the direction of the Schanifeld. He couldn't see it from where he stood, but he knew it waited, whispering with Moltod and Leycie's prayers. If he built his Citadel, he would see it every day, and Moltod would see his devotion. This was his chance to create a new future. Not the one written by Leycie, not to continue the life of a cobbler's son, but as lord.

And an architect.

He turned back to his father. "Very well. When do I begin?"

FOUR

The Goryl Family provided Alojzy with sixteen workers, two mages, and an empty property on the edge of the Schanifeld. With his blueprints in hand, each morning, Alojzy said goodbye to his parents and ventured to the southern edge of town where his workers gathered.

It was strange, having this power over the workers; even the mages, two elderly magic users who had long been loyal to the Goryl Family, listened to his every move. He was wary of giving the mages too much work, worried they might place a hex or curse on his new Citadel in the name of Leycie. An older worker reassured him that would not be the case; one mage molded stone to their will, while the other controlled the weather—neither of these would lead to curses or hexes. But it did not keep Alojzy's worry at bay. There was something about magic that made him wary; after all, didn't magic only belong to Moltod and Leycie? Why should a simple human control and manipulate nature?

Throughout the construction, he gave the mages simple tasks: acquire decorative stone, keep the sun in the sky, and send reports back to the Goryl Family.

With the mages under hand, Alojzy worked with pride in his chest. He could see his castle coming to fruition before him. It started as nothing more than a wall, but almost in a blink, he saw his own drawings jump out of the page. The workers took his idea and brought it to life.

Almost like they had magic themselves.

Yet as Alojzy's Citadel grew, so did the constant nagging of his future marriage to Dobroslawa Goryl. It didn't really occur to him that he'd pledged his life to a woman he'd never met.

At least, not until the day she showed up outside the half-built wall of his masterpiece.

He'd only seen her once from afar, but he recognized her as soon as she arrived on the back of a black horse with an entourage of warriors behind her. She bore a certain essence around her when she landed on the ground. Everyone stopped their work. Even Alojzy looked up from his blueprints to stare in awe. She wasn't beautiful, but she walked with pride, her body strong and steps determined. She was a tall, slender woman with dirty blonde hair— the Goryl genes ran deep into her blood. And she carried on her shoulders the ongoing fight against Kainan.

Dobroslawa approached Alojzy with a determined stride. A couple of her warriors followed in step. Alojzy noted a burly fellow at her side with a thick blond beard, but when Dobroslawa waved her hand, he and the others all stepped away from her.

"Are you Mr. Gorski?" she asked.

Alojzy bowed. "Dame Goryl. It is a pleasure to meet at last."

She eyed the surrounding area. "Is this the castle you are building with my parents' money?"

Alojzy followed her gaze. "Yes. This shall be our home in three years, after our wedding."

She approached one of the half-built walls and grazed her fingertips over the stone. Alojzy couldn't quite read her; she wore her emotions tight to her chest, and any flinch in her eyes could be nothing more than the flicker of the sun.

Her next statement bore no emotion. "It appears this will be quite the monument."

"But of course," Alojzy replied. "For our god, Moltod."

"Yes, for Moltod." Dobroslawa closed her eyes. "Of course, for Moltod."

"Does this not please you?" Alojzy's stomach twisted. The mere thought of Dobroslawa returning to her parents and ridiculing his work sent his mind into a flurry. Would they take away his funding? Take away the property? Would he have to worship Moltod alone in the forest again, just as he had as an adolescent?

No. He wouldn't let that happen. This was his project, his ambition, and his pride.

The Citadel belonged to him.

Dobroslawa glanced down at Alojzy, then managed a slight smile. "I am only worried that when we marry, we shall lose each other in these halls."

The weight vanished from Alojzy's shoulders, and he even smiled back at Dobroslawa. "Do not worry. I have already taken that worry into account. Come, see." He motioned her back to his drafting table. "See, look. I have already segregated the entire eastern tower as our living space."

"What is the rest for?"

"The central keep will be for Moltod, and the western tower will be a place for troops and others to rest...and pray." Alojzy flipped through a few more pages of his draft, then motioned with his chin towards the workers. "We are currently digging out the basement floors for the servants and for the galley. I can promise you I have planned everything meticulously so our home will be more than a castle; it will be our utopia."

Dobroslawa glanced over at the drafts on the table. Her long fingers traced the outline of the galley's design. "Very nice."

"I was hoping it would please you."

"It does, but..." She stepped back. "I was wondering if I may look over the plans and make suggestions? If this is to be my home as well, I would like to make sure it has everything I need as well."

"You do not trust my judgment?"

"I do, of course, and I doubt I will make many changes. But a second pair of eyes can turn something excellent into something...well...fantastic." She smiled again.

Alojzy stared at his drafts again. These sketches had been *his* project. Why should Dobroslawa come in and rewrite everything?

But her family funded the project, and she was to be his wife, so he had no other option.

"Of course, Dame Goryl. I can have copies produced for you at once."

"Thank you, Mr. Gorski." Dobroslawa held her hand out to him. "To our continued union."

Alojzy slowly took her blistered hand and shook it. "To our union indeed."

FIVE

Dobroslawa became a fixture at the construction site. At first, Alojzy tried to avoid her, but every day, she sought him out with a determined stride. Each time, she carried notes on his sketches with new requests and recommendations. Alojzy took them with a kind "thank you" but didn't dare look at them until she had long left the site.

In his small bedroom back home, he would pour over her notes. He tossed over half of them into the fire, most of the requests petty, regarding the color or shape of a room. A few recommendations went against Moltod; why build a hospital or a school in *their* own home? Their Citadel was for Moltod and their future family. No one else.

Some of Dobroslawa's recommendations left an impact on Alojzy: building a private library, incorporating multiple private offices for their own work, and adding a nursery for their future children.

He kept a few suggestions close, all while keeping his future wife at arm's length. She only crossed his mind as an annoyance while his heart and soul bled for this castle. At night, he prayed to Moltod for success, for keeping the evil mages away, and for his workers' health. Some nights, he asked Moltod to keep Dobroslawa from sabotaging his work, and some days, Moltod listened.

Towards the end of the project, war called Dobroslawa back to the battlefields. Alojzy watched from the top of the near-finished Citadel as the battalion marched into the Schanifeld. He smirked to himself, thanking Moltod for the much-needed distraction.

Now, he could build his castle in peace.

Alojzy finished his Citadel one moon phase before the day of his wedding. It rose from the ground, a behemoth on the landscape. Foes would fear it as they approached. But the castle really belonged in a museum. Every element shone, from the carefully placed stones of each wall to the green and bustling courtyard amongst the towers. The two towers on either side of the courtyard belonged to the stars.

Alojzy's shining joy, above all else, was the Keep. Placed in the heart of the Citadel, the Keep served as his permanent altar to Moltod. With carvings of the headless god on either side of the door, whenever he entered it, Alojzy swore Moltod watched him. Paintings of Moltod's loyal angels, in long robes and dark eyes, decorated the glass, their bodies surrounded by abstract and smoke. An altar, a mini castle itself, waited in a mirage of smoke at the center of the Keep. Candles lined the aisles. Shadows flickered on the wall, creating fake movement, as if the Keep itself changed depending on Moltod's mood.

Every time Alojzy entered the Keep, he mumbled a prayer to Moltod before pricking his finger. A drop of blood fell from his finger and landed on the altar.

Let you create something by my sacrifice. Alojzy watched as the blood seeped into the stone, then left the Keep beneath Moltod's gaze.

When not in the Keep, Alojzy walked the halls of the rest of the towers. He passed by servants from the Goryl household as they brought in different pieces of furniture and decorated the walls with the family crest. They bowed to him as he walked, respecting him as if he were already part of the family. He would smile, then turn away with a scowl. The Goryl family crest mocked him. While the Goryl family provided the funding, in the end, wasn't this his castle?

Whether or not they liked it, once the servants left, he removed one of the golden Goryl crests with the Dame Boguslawa Goryl in its center. She stared at him, sword in her hand, eyes dark and focused. As he removed it, he paused, glaring down at the woman.

"You have enough pride," he whispered, then carried it over to the window and tossed it down into the Schanifeld.

The pieces shattered amongst the black and white tulips.

Alojzy turned his back on the broken crest and walked back over to the wall. From his bag on the floor, he removed the crest he'd been sketching for years. Embossed in silver, a single figure sat in a chair, sword in its hand.

The figure bore no head, only a single flower sprouting from its neck.

SIX

On the day of the wedding, it snowed. If Alojzy worshiped Leycie, he might have worried.

But with Moltod beside him, he celebrated.

Rather than having their wedding in the Citadel's courtyard, they moved the ceremony into the Keep, beneath the altar of Moltod.

Alojzy stood at the altar, dressed in his black robe, with both his parents in their white robes beside him. He nodded at his parents. His mother's eyes fell, and his father squirmed. They'd never stood this close to the altar of Moltod; in fact, this was the first time they'd dare step foot in his Citadel. Since building his castle, he'd grown more distant from them.

Five years since he began, he was a different man.

Five years spent, and his parents had become strangers.

A priest from town joined them at the altar next, carrying a bottle of bier and two glasses, which he placed at the altar. The priest wore a robe of gray, a color reminiscent of both Leycie and Moltod, a union of peace. The warriors of Evylain bore the same color, though Alojzy often wondered, what were they defending if not aligned with one God?

All the guests wore equally neutral colors. The shining pride of the ceremony, as bright as the moon in the sky, was Moltod.

And with his shining light, he guided Dobroslawa into the Keep.

Even Alojzy admitted Dobroslawa looked stunning in her black robes dotted with flakes of snow. She had combed her hair back, and cosmetics caked her face. Her parents walked beside her, one dressed in black and one in white. Dobroslawa stared at the ground, only to raise her head as she passed a few of the guests. The four women in the front row bore Dobroslawa's green eyes and thin lips, their familial resemblance proud. Yet, Dobroslawa did not look at them but at the row of soldiers behind them: her squadron. Alojzy had seen them come and go from the Citadel during construction, always Dobroslawa's loyal steeds.

That would have to change.

Dobroslawa held her gaze the longest with a bearded man Alojzy had met a couple years earlier. The gaze lasted only a few seconds but long enough for Alojzy to notice.

Before anyone else noticed, she snapped her head forward and joined Alojzy at the altar. Their parents stepped back as she bowed to Alojzy, so her head fell lower than his eyes. He waited for his emotions to bubble, to swell to the forefront of his mind and embrace him. But he felt nothing for her. Not when he held Moltod in his heart.

Despite the years of work building this castle, not a single pang of love entered his heart. She was a means to an end, a chance to build his castle. What if he banished her from his home? What if he claimed the castle his and his alone?

The soldiers in the room would outnumber him at once. Alojzy knew his strength; he knew he was nothing more than a stout, weak man who used mind over mass to fight his battles.

Time would be his friend. His castle would thrive, and he would be its master.

Nerves didn't take him. He moved through the motions of the marriage ceremony, merely raising his hand and placing it on Dobroslawa's forehead. She stayed in her spot for a moment. Then, in the traditional act, she rose to her feet, letting his hand slide off her forehead so she could catch it and press it to her mouth.

"A union, some say, is the end," the priest said, "But for Leycie and Moltod, it was the beginning of something new. It was the beginning of peace and prosperity, of life and of death, and of light and of dark. It unified abstract with absolute and imagination with reality. This is what a marriage holds. It is what the union of Herr Alojzy Gorski and Dame Dobroslawa Goryl will hold. Unless, of course, anyone sees this union as tarnishing the legacy behind them."

No one spoke.

"As it must be." The priest turned to Alojzy and opened his hands. "She is yours."

Alojzy took Dobroslawa's hand and raised her palm to his lips. Sweat kissed him back.

He restrained his scowl.

The priest turned back to Dobroslawa as Alojzy straightened his back. "He is yours."

Dobroslawa performed the same ritual. A kiss of the palm, and a release.

The priest then took both their hands and held them close to his chest. "So it must be. And so it is. A wedding, a union, as one."

He then released their hands and turned to the altar. With a whisper on his lips, he uttered a prayer to Moltod, then poured two glasses of bier.

He handed one to Alojzy and one to Dobroslawa.

Alojzy linked his gaze with his wife's. Then, in a single motion, they raised their glasses and took a swig.

SEVEN

Dobroslawa moved into the castle like a quiet rain. At first, Alojzy hardly noticed her. They would join each other for mealtime and behind closed doors for bed. Otherwise, Dobroslawa spent much of her time in the barracks with her soldiers while Alojzy placed the final touches on the castle.

The first night of their marriage, they established these boundaries.

During the reception after the ceremony, they sat side-by-side, not touching, while forcing their smiles. They danced once, and afterwards, Alojzy joined his workers to discuss the remaining work on the Citadel while Dobroslawa joined her squadron. She spoke with them, her laughter warm in the room. Alojzy's throat tightened when she placed a hand on the shoulder of that large man with the thick blond beard.

Alojzy considered mentioning it to Dobroslawa as they left the reception together. He bit his tongue, though, guiding her instead to the bedroom and silently wielding his new power as her husband.

Despite the limited love between Alojzy and his wife, they found passion in bed. He looked forward to the nights when he could unwrap her clothes. She was vulnerable then, no longer masked by a layer of armor. In bed, he was the ruler; she was nothing more than his patron.

During the day, Alojzy focused on his castle. He repainted walls, repositioned his crest, and planned the final details to fortify his home. Soldiers came and went while patrons of Moltod visited the Keep. The servants, gifted to him and Dobroslawa on their wedding day, bowed to him. He was no longer a cobbler and a soldier's son; he was a lord of a castle, a man of respect.

His routine became redundant, though. It felt like Moltod slipped through his fingers, and the unpredictable vanished. Leycie must have been weaving her hands through the temple. Was he doing something wrong? Was there something amiss?

He welcomed the change in routine one day when Dobroslawa found him in the hallway.

"Herr Gorski," she approached him. "May we talk?"

"At this hour, Lady Goryl?" he inquired.

"I believe it is important."

Alojzy motioned for his wife to follow him into his private library. He ran his fingers along the books before sitting down at the desk. Dobroslawa fidgeted slightly, picking at the edge of the desk as she took a seat. The mask of confidence she wore often had fallen away, leaving behind a woman at Alojzy's mercy.

"What do you wish to speak about?" Alojzy asked.

She licked her lips, then said, "I would like to request additional quarters for my squadron."

"I have already told you, we are not a castle to harbor soldiers, but for passing by and training. This is Moltod's Citadel."

"Yes, I know...but I would at least like to keep rooms here for my three commanders."

"Which three are those again?"

"Commander Miran Bilyk, Commander Natalya Novak, and Commander Szyman Gutnik."

Alojzy knew those names, but one remained embedded in his mind. "Szyman Gutnik... Is that the big fellow?"

After the incident at the wedding, where he saw Dobroslawa with the big hairy fellow, he had a servant to investigate. While the servant found no evidence of a relationship or companionship between the two, Alojzy remained wary. Even if he harbored no love for Dobroslawa, ultimately, she was his wife.

"Yes, our mage," Dobroslawa replied. "Very talented. He has helped us win many battles."

Alojzy sucked on his lips. Could he trust another mage? It had taken everything to trust the two who helped build the Citadel. While they ultimately did no wrong, a weight fell from Alojzy when they left.

"What is his magic?" Alojzy asked.

"He creates mirages of cities and campsites. We have distracted many Kainan soldiers with his fallacies." Dobroslawa raised her hands. "I promise, he is not malicious in the slightest. But it could prove useful if the Kainan army ever attacks from the north. He could create mirages of another Citadel and mask this one. Think about the strategic benefits. Even if this is not a castle for war, they will target it, Alojzy. Kainan soldiers know no difference."

Alojzy rose and paced the room, hands laced behind his back. "Yes, I see your point. But counterpoint: if the Kainan army discovers we harbor a powerful army in this castle, then they will see Freiborn as a target."

"The squadron already trains here, so what difference does it make? If they are not here, they are elsewhere in Freiborn. Please, Alojzy. I am asking for three rooms for my friends and confidantes. They will not interfere with your part of the castle. It will only make my life easier if they are here."

"What does it matter if they are here or down the road? You have feet, Dame Goryl. You can walk."

"Yes, I can, but I fear it might compromise my health for the next few months."

"Explain."

She fidgeted with her hands again, then caught Alojzy's eyes. "As my husband, you are the first to know: I have missed two months of bleeding. Without a doubt, I am pregnant."

The tension released from Alojzy's shoulders. A smile twitched on his lips. *Moltod, thank you.*

He took his wife's hand. "Now I understand your request, and if you ask for it, so it shall be. At least until the child is born. For your health and their health matters the most."

Dobroslawa smiled at him. "I appreciate your support."

"It is only my duty. So it must be."

EIGHT

Dobroslawa's pregnancy ended Leycie's plague of redundancy. Moltod's presence returned with force, and Alojzy's pride once again thrived.

Despite his initial reservations, he allowed for Dobroslawa's commanders to maintain residency in the west tower. He had no qualms with Miran or Natalya, but his attention constantly fell on the mage known as Szyman. About five years older than Alojzy, his presence dominated the Citadel. Large, with a heavy step, it was hard to miss him in the dining hall. Even though Szyman talked little, when he did, his voice boomed. Alojzy cringed whenever his deep voice rang through the halls.

"Al!" he called one morning from down the hall, "I have an inquiry for you."

Alojzy froze, straining his facial muscles to form a smile as he turned. "Szyman, what is it this time?"

"Have I really asked you for so much already?"

"You asked for enough." Already the man had requested a thicker mattress for his back and a room on the top floor with a view of the Schanifeld. It required Alojzy to reconfigure exactly where everything went, and while he believed in breaking and rearranging order, he yearned for control over the chaos. "Are your quarters not to your liking?"

"Oh, yes, the quarters are perfect. It is nothing of major importance there." Szyman chuckled that loud, annoying laugh.

"Then what is your inquiry?" Alojzy hissed.

"Only a request. I have a friend who travels quite a bit...and some days, she is weary and needs a place to stay."

"I gave quarters to Dame Goryl's commanders. There are no more rooms," Alojzy stated.

"Oh, I was not asking for that. She can sleep in my room."

"So, she is your lover?"

"Oh, no. More like...an older sister." He chuckled again. "I only wanted to make sure it was okay that she stayed. If you were to run into her, I would hate to have guards sent after her."

Alojzy cracked his neck and relaxed his shoulders. "Very well. What is her name?"

"Her name is Malaika. Chances are, you won't even see her. She comes and goes in silence and as she pleases."

"Very well. I will inform the guards not to harm this...Malaika." He tasted the name on his tongue. "Is that a foreign name?"

"Yes. She has moved around quite a bit. I believe she hails from the western continent."

"I see." Alojzy turned. "Well, that is all good, but I have other matters to attend to. I promised Dame Goryl I would bring her a midday meal."

Szyman fell into step with Alojzy. "Would you like me to bring her food? I know her pregnancy has been a difficult one, and I would love a chance to confide in a friend."

Alojzy considered Szyman's offer. He needed time to work on the new drafting request for the Nachtnebel Family's treasury. But the idea of Szyman kneeling down beside his wife, giving her whatever her heart demanded, gave him pause.

"It is fine. I can bring her food. She is my wife, after all."

"May I come with you at least? She is my friend, and I miss her."

Alojzy narrowed his eyes at Szyman. He wanted nothing more than to break the man's neck, but he was bigger than Alojzy on all counts. Even after years of building the castle, Alojzy built little muscle mass. He was a tad shorter than average, with Szyman's hulking stature dwarfing him. Generally, Alojzy had no resentment of larger men. He made up for it all in his skill set and prayer. But now, he wished he had a way to best the man standing before him.

"She is my wife, Herr Gutnik. She is not yours."

"I—"

"You are welcome to stay here. You are welcome to bring your friends and ladies back to your room. But she is *my* wife. Remember that." He prodded Szyman in the chest with a firm finger. "Remember, I rule this castle. Not you."

NINE

A lojzy and Dobroslawa welcomed twin girls in the heart of summer. They chose the names Celina and Elzbieta for the girls, and for the first year of their life, Alojzy devoted every passing moment to them. He built them a nursery fit for two princesses, filled with toys and dresses from the finest vendors across the city. He imagined a day when he could teach them how to build with blocks and show them the stories of Leycie and Moltod.

Yet, by the end of their first year, Alojzy's infatuation with his new daughters waned. Despite the break from routine, their incessant babbling and screaming no longer warmed his heart.

Each day, he watched from a distance, taking a step back each time the full moon lit up the sky. From afar, he watched.

He took his furthest step back one day as he watched them play. Celina, the larger of the two girls, reached forward and grabbed Elzbieta's blonde hair. The scream that exited her sister shook the room.

"Celina!" Dobroslawa raced over from beside Alojzy. "Don't you see that pulling Elzbieta's hair harms her?"

The infant stared at her mother with wide brown eyes.

Alojzy grumbled. As his daughters grew, only their eye color showed any resemblance to him. With their mother's fair skin and a head of golden locks, no one would have thought him to be their father.

They look like Szyman. The thought came like a whisper but remained echoing like thunder.

"Alojzy, could you carry Elzbieta? The girls need some time apart," Dobroslawa called over her shoulder.

Sighing, Alojzy lifted the smaller infant off the ground. The child squirmed.

"Stop it. Now!" he ordered.

"Alojzy, that's not how to talk to her!" Dobroslawa spat.

"Well, she needs to learn to listen."

"She is barely a year old."

"Now is as good a time as any."

"That's preposterous." Dobroslawa positioned Celina on one hip. "Give her to me if you are going to be ridiculous about this."

Alojzy huffed and passed the child to his wife. She positioned both infants on her hips, and with a glare, she stormed from the room as if on her way to war.

"Oh, what did I do this time?" Alojzy called after her, lacing his hands behind his back as he kept her in stride.

"You were such a good father the first couple months. What happened?" she asked, not looking in his direction.

Alojzy shrugged, once again eyeing his daughters' blonde curls. "I am tired."

"You do not think I am tired too? I sacrificed my command for these girls. The least you could do is put the same love into them as you do your Citadel."

"I give them plenty of love."

"*Things* are not love. Any follower of Moltod knows that love is a product of—"

"I know what Moltod thinks of love," Alojzy said under his breath.

Dobroslawa turned to face him, readjusting the girls again in her arms. "Tell me. What does he say?"

"Love is a product of abstract and adventure, not of routine and ordinary."

"And love is a product of connection. Both Leycie and Moltod say that." Dobroslawa stepped forward. "Connect with your daughters, Alojzy. They are your blood."

The next words slipped out of Alojzy's mouth before he knew they were going to: "Are they, though?"

"Pardon?"

"Their hair does not resemble our hair. In fact...I'd say they have your commander's hair."

"You mean Szyman?" Dobroslawa's nostrils flared, eyes narrowed. "Are you accusing me of having an affair?"

"I've seen you with him."

"I've known him since I was a child! He is like a brother to me! I would never share a bed with him."

"Why should I believe you?" Alojzy pressured.

"Because I am your wife. I know my duty. I would never tarnish our legacy. These daughters are yours, Alojzy. No one else."

"Then explain the hair."

Dobroslawa laughed. "Alojzy, curls run in my family! When I was a little girl, I had curly blonde hair. It darkened after I cut it short and I covered my head with armor. Ask my mother and father. They will tell you it is true."

Alojzy straightened his back and clenched his hands together while his gaze turned to the window overlooking the Schanifeld. "Very well."

"I hope you can find other ways to occupy your mind now. Your daughters need a father." With that, Dobroslawa left with Celina and Elzbieta, her boots clanking down the hall. She disappeared into the nursery, leaving Alojzy alone with his thoughts.

He grumbled to himself and began his stride towards the Keep. How dare Dobroslawa try to fool him! There was no way those children were not Szyman's. The two were clearly lovers, hiding in the halls of the Citadel. But other than the curly hair of his daughters, he had no proof. Dobroslawa might claim she had curly hair as a child, but none of the other Goryl girls had hair like his daughters. Even his nieces and nephews all bore the straight, dusty locks of the Goryl family. Perhaps it had been a genetic twist, but he knew deep in his heart that Szyman and Dobroslawa had a connection.

He placed his hand against a stone and sighed. What would the Citadel tell him if it could talk? Would it show him the truth? Why couldn't he see through its eyes? Then, he wouldn't stand in place, asking questions he couldn't answer. He'd be able to focus on his work, sketching out new architectural plans while reading books in devotion to Moltod. Instead, his daughters' existence nagged at him.

He took a step forward, eyes still downcast on the stone floors.

Thud!

A figure slammed into his body. He stumbled backward, glowering down at it. A short, dark woman with frizzy hair stood before him. She wore an old scout uniform, long retired from years ago, with a sword on her hip. In her hand, she carried a yellow-filled jar.

In Moltod's name... What is this girl doing with a jar of honey?

"Have you not learned to watch where you are going?" Alojzy snapped at the woman.

She blinked, holding the jar close.

"Speak when addressed, girl." The woman might have been about Alojzy's age, if not older, but he would have none of these missteps in *his* castle. He was the master; everyone else might as well have been a child.

"Apologies. I'm gonna see my friend," she blurted.

"With a jar of honey?"

"Oh, no, this isn't honey. It's...lemon marmalade that I got in Rosada. I promised my friend he could try it."

"This is not a public forum for exchanges."

"But I'm allowed to be here!"

"Oh?"

"Yes! You allowed me!"

"I have never met you."

"But I'm Malaika—Szyman's friend. You must be Herr Gorski! Sorry. I didn't mean to barge into you like this. Just so used to people ignoring me and all." She chuckled to herself. "You're not how I pictured you!"

"And how did Szyman describe me?" Alojzy asked.

"Well, the way he talked about you, I kinda pictured some tall man with a full head of luscious hair."

Alojzy frowned, running his fingers through his already thinning hair.

"But I'd like to say how sorry I am, y'know. Really. Shoulda looked where I was going. Really sorry, Herr Gorski...really!"

"If you are actually sorry, you will leave my sight at once."

"Thank you, Herr Gorski. Sorry again!" Malaika darted off down the hall, nearly tripping over her feet as she stopped herself from turning right into the Galley. There, she spun around, heading left towards the barracks.

Alojzy had completely forgotten about Szyman's friend. His entire time in the Citadel, he hadn't seen the girl once. What secrets was she spreading? Were she and Szyman planning something?

His feet carried him after the strange woman and towards the barracks. Alojzy rarely visited the eastern tower, but he still had the inside of it memorized. A set of prison cells waited empty in the basement. They had no prisoners, with the Schanifeld remaining empty and untarnished for the past two years. But men and women continued to practice their sword fighting in the long empty halls while the occasional soldier stayed the night before heading out to war. Each of Dobroslawa's three commanders had a room near the top of the eastern tower. He rarely saw Merin and Natalya, but Szyman remained a constant presence.

At the top of the tower, Alojzy pressed himself against the wall, watching as that Malaika girl knocked on Szyman's door. The door cracked open, and once she slipped inside, Alojzy snuck over to the door and pressed his ear against the wall.

"Here, here, take this," Malaika said on the other side of the door.

"A jar of...marmalade?" Szyman asked.

"No, it's something worse."

"I never heard someone call marmalade bad."

"I hate marmalade, but that's nothing. Listen, I need you to keep this safe. They won't know to find it."

"I told you I don't want any part in this." Szyman hissed.

Part of what? Alojzy pressed his ear hard against the wall.

"I know. I am working to keep them off your trail," Malaika said. "Perhaps if I find another one, they'll forget about you."

"Where are you going to find another one like me?"

"Well, I just ran into one. If there are two right here in this castle, then I'm willing to bet there's a bunch of them out there."

Of what? Alojzy prayed to Moltod for an answer to come.

"Multiple? Are you sure?" Szyman replied.

"Makes sense, doesn't it?"

"Perhaps...but..." Szyman paused, then lowered his voice, "Who did you run into?"

"That stingy lord, Alojzy. He's really not all that grand, is he?"

"Don't say that about him. He is quite smart—"

"Smart doesn't mean he's got looks."

Alojzy flared his nostrils.

"I think that is beside the point."

"You're right, it is. But what I'm saying is, if he saw me, that means he's either one of us, or he's a seer. But you said he's shown no magic, right?"

"He hates mages. Doesn't trust them."

"Then he's one of us. Whether he knows it or not."

One of what!? Alojzy restrained the urge to scream. If he made any noise, Szyman would discover him. He could almost imagine the man snapping him in two, then letting the Malaika girl stab him thrice with her sword.

"Are you going to...pursue him?" Szyman asked.

"Nah, not until I know if there are others. Rather pick from the best than some stout lord of a castle."

Alojzy grunted.

"Then I shall not mention a word to him."

"Good," Malaika said. "And you'll keep this thing safe, right?"

"Will you at least tell me what it is?"

Malaika paused. If she answered, Alojzy didn't hear. Even Szyman's booming voice had grown as quiet as a mouse.

Alojzy stepped away from the door and started his slow descent back down the tower.

Yet, his mind spun; there was something wicked occurring in his Citadel. He couldn't be sure if it had to do with magic, with the newcomer, or with his wife. Whatever it was, it had to do with *him*. He was *something*.

For now, he would wait.

Patience would reward him.

TEN

Alojzy moved his private library to the far side of the western tower, where he could look over the courtyard and the barracks. He spent his days watching from the window like a hawk, paying only half a mind to his different architectural designs. Often, he daydreamed while struggling to reach his deadlines. His employers sent message after message to him, requesting the blueprints. Somehow he always finished, even if he didn't remember how, but his employers never seemed satisfied. Even with their threats of finding a different architect, Alojzy still could not pull his attention away from the window.

His attention loitered over Szyman. Alojzy often cornered him in the halls to inquire about his friend Malaika. The man gave simple answers, and even when

Alojzy raised the question of magic, his trained response was what every mage said: "Our magic comes from Leycie and Moltod. There are those of earth and life, and there are those of mist and death. Moltod powers my magic."

"You imply that your magic comes from Moltod... does that make you one of his angels?" Alojzy asked.

"You know as well as I do that Moltod's angels are dead souls."

Alojzy knew that Szyman was right, but he continued to pressure the man. Szyman would say no more. Once, he offered a demonstration of his magic.

Alojzy accepted the offer only one time. In the courtyard, with a wave of his hand, Szyman created a replica of a small house he'd seen on the outside of town. If Alojzy had known none better, he would have thought it to be real.

Besides the spectacle, Alojzy received no answers. So, he continued his quiet sentinel, waiting for Malaika to return.

He always felt a tension rise from his shoulders whenever Szyman left to conduct deceptive spells against the Kainan opposition on the Schanifeld. It was in those moments he thought he might reconnect with his wife. But he never did.

Truthfully, he'd grown even more distant from his wife with each month passing and fewer words exchanged. They still ate dinner every night, and as their daughters grew, those evening meals became the only familial bonds they shared. Each time he took a gander at his daughters, they seemed at least half a foot taller, their dark eyes more knowledgeable. As Dobroslawa claimed, their curls eventually straightened, and their hair darkened. But that did little to quell his suspicions. Whenever they laughed, it reminded him of Szyman. The way they smiled, it might as well have been his mouth. Alojzy could not shake it and rather kept his distance, studying as his girls grew from infants, to children, to adolescents.

He cared little about what Dobroslawa did with her time. Once the girls had grown older, she returned to her duties amongst her soldiers, venturing off into the Schanifeld as her duty entailed. With her gone, he ventured to one of the taverns on the edge of Freiborn, taking stock of pleasures and vices while listening to the drunken soldiers tell their tales. Sometimes, men of Kainan would enter the taverns, but in the musk of bier and sweat, no one batted an eye.

Once again in their presence, Alojzy transported himself back to the woods, spying on the soldiers. Here, in the tavern, he listened more to the men about their god, about land abroad in Kainan, and of their travel. These men might have been the enemy, but their stories held similarities to his own; they devoted themselves to Moltod and ruled their castles as kings.

While Alojzy kept to a quiet corner to watch and listen, he absorbed the warrior's words. A common theme remained: do not stay in the shadows and build your future, one stone at a time.

When home, the words bubbled into Alojzy's mind, dancing between each of his thoughts. He spent hours pacing and watching the towers, unable to focus on his blueprints. Each architectural design grew more cumbersome, his work turning from prestige to mediocre. No matter how many hours he spent working, nothing matched the plans he'd laid out for his Citadel.

But as time turned, and Moltod did not reopen the doors of creativity, even Alojzy's Citadel turned bland.

The altar in the Keep no longer glistened. As he prayed each evening to Moltod, it didn't feel like Moltod listened. Rather, an incessant hum filled the room, leaving him with a pocket of annoyance and not a sense of enlightenment.

Was this what it meant to get older? To lose the spark and forget what made his heart shine?

He'd already built his pride and joy; what else could he do?

Some days, standing in his tower, he pondered what might happen if he jumped from the window onto the ground. Would people mourn his death? Would his parents finally enter his Citadel again after avoiding it for years? Would Dobroslawa admit to what she did wrong? Perhaps his death would be the catalyst allowing them to embrace Moltod.

But he didn't have the heart to jump, and each day he returned to his drafting table.

Panic replaced his focus. He stared for hours at the drafting table, willing for his sketches to take form. The pages remained blank.

He cursed under his breath. Why wouldn't the ideas come anymore? Why did his thoughts continue to focus on that Szyman and his friend Malaika? Why wouldn't Moltod just let his thoughts behave?

Alojzy slammed his fist on the table. The candle fell onto its side, catching the drafting paper up in flame. He raced to put it out, suffocating the fire with the sleeve of his shirt. The smoke remained, like a cloud of smoke left behind from a demolition. As he brushed it away, his mind went to the new treasury for the Nacht-nebel Family that he promised to design nearly two years early. Freiborn had ordered the old treasury's demolition; a drab building without windows, mold made itself at home within the walls. Alojzy imagined a golden maze-like castle as its replacement, where deep beneath the ground, the greatest riches of the town resided.

They needed the plans by the end of the month. But he couldn't design it with only a few days remaining.

What could he do?

The smoke from the candle cleared.

He blinked.

On the table, an exact miniature replica of his imagined treasury sat before him. It hung there, surrounded by mist, before settling down on the drafting paper. In a blink, it merged with the paper, a complete draft that had haunted him for months on end.

"What in the name of Moltod..." He touched the page and cringed. *Magic...* The word echoed in his thoughts. He glanced around the room, then out into the hallway. No one loitered.

Alone, as always.

He returned to his table and stared at the draft before him.

"Moltod has answered my blessings then..." he waved his fingers through the last bits of drifting smoke. This time, another small castle appeared, only to fade after a moment.

"Thank you," he whispered out the window to the Schanifeld, "You shall not regret this."

ELEVEN

Alojzy practiced with this new blessing of magic in private. He built small fixtures on his table before letting them seep into the drafting paper. His employers no longer badgered him, and one stressor fell from his shoulders. Yet, he didn't know the limitations of this magic. At one point, he even considered asking Szyman. The man's magic appeared similar, but with a caveat: Szyman replicated that which existed, all the while, Alojzy could create as well.

He didn't need that traitorous man to tell him anything.

Alojzy spent even more time away from his family. He stopped going to the taverns, locking himself in his private library for days. With a wave of his hand, he built miniature towns, drafted sprawling libraries, and reconstructed his Citadel.

Did this have to do with what he heard Malaika say those years ago? She and Szyman spoke of magic and of Alojzy... but what did that mean?

He made it his mission to corner the woman.

Yet, Malaika returned only three times over the course of the years, as far as Alojzy knew. Despite telling the guards to look out for her return, no one ever reported her arrival. It left Alojzy to watch for the odd woman. Twice he saw her as she left the Citadel, cloak over her curly hair, blending in with the night sky. He tried chasing after her, but before he reached the courtyard, she had already faded into the fog falling over the Schanifeld.

The third time, he saw her enter the Citadel.

Late into the evening, as he sat at his drafting table surrounded by books about an old library, he glimpsed the gates opening. Alojzy rose at once and peered out the window. Malaika snuck into the Citadel like a mouse, creeping along the courtyard towards the eastern tower. She didn't look from the ground, but Alojzy recognized her short stature and unkempt curls at once. Without hesitating, he rushed out of his drafting studio and down into the courtyard.

She'd already vanished into the eastern tower by the time Alojzy reached the courtyard. He had no time to wait. After years, he would finally corner her and ask what she meant all those years ago; why did she speak of him as if he were something inhuman?

Alojzy rushed into the barracks and up the stairs. At the end of the hall, the door to Szyman's room opened and shut. He hurried towards it, instantly pressing himself against the wall to listen as Malaika spoke with Szyman.

"You still have it, right?" Malaika asked in a rushed tone.

"I have not moved it from the wall," Szyman replied.

Scuffling echoed from the other side of the wall, followed by the clatter of objects on the floor. He held his breath.

"What is it, Malaika?" Szyman asked.

"I'm concerned they might know where I am hiding it."

"I thought you said—"

"And I haven't told them about you! But they've figured out that there's another one of ya'll here. They've noticed something, and I think they want me to pursue him."

"You mean Al?"

"Yeah, Al-man. Alojzy or whatever you call him."

"Call him Al. It annoys him." Szyman chuckled.

Alojzy flared his nostrils.

Malaika continued rambling. "Yeah, but he seems like a stuck-up twat. I'd rather not train him. So, I think it's best I take that right there and get it outta here. I'd hate to put you in an awkward position."

"I've almost figured out how to keep it safe, though." Szyman objected. "Here, we can head out to the Schanifeld. I'll show you."

"Okay... but we gotta be quick about it."

The doorknob to the room turned. Alojzy clenched his fists, willing himself to stay in place.

Szyman stepped out into the hallways with Malaika on his heels. She held that jar from years ago in her hands, with the same yellow substance filling the container.

Alojzy stepped out in front of them. "Finally."

"Al! What're you doing here?" Szyman stumbled back from him.

"I want answers." He glowered at Szyman, then at Malaika.

"About what?"

"About everything."

"What?"

"I heard everything. About me. About that jar. Explain."

"You eavesdropped!? That's quite rude!" Malaika interjected.

"You are staying in my castle. Anything you say, I can know."

"Well, it is none of your business. Now excuse me." Malaika pushed past him.

Alojzy grabbed her arm. "I suggest you talk, or I'll throw you in one of our cells."

"Wouldn't matter." Malaika struggled in his grasp.

"Oh? It'd make an example out of you. The first person in eleven years to get thrown into my Citadel's prison...it would be a historic event."

"Nah. Not worth it."

"Oh?"

"Yeah, not at all." She clutched the jar of supposed marmalade in her hand, then raised it over her head, "Szyman! Catch!"

The jar flew. Szyman caught it in one large hand, then darted past Alojzy and down the hall, his heavy footsteps echoing against the stone.

"Choose your answers, Alojzy," Malaika stated.

Alojzy glowered down at Malaika, then down the hall. He cursed and dropped the woman's arm.

Alojzy made his choice and raced after Szyman. He wouldn't let that man get away; he should have thrown him in the prison cells years ago. But no, he respected his wife's wishes. He no longer would...assuming he could catch Szyman. Yet Szyman was larger and faster than him, and already the man had reached the stair-well. He wouldn't be able to catch up to Szyman on foot.

Rather, Alojzy slowed down by a window overlooking the courtyard. He had little time to think. So, he didn't.

Instead, he jumped.

The ground came fast. As he fell, he prayed to Moltod to raise the ground to a higher level. Was it not just the same as when he built his miniature castles? Instead, he rebuilt the ground. He landed on his hands and knees within seconds. Rather than falling six stories, he only fell two, and as he pulled himself up, the ground low-ered itself to its usual height. He survived, despite the cracking in his left hand. He didn't sit around waiting for the pain to dissipate, instead gathering himself on his feet and racing to the entrance of the east tower.

As Szyman exited the tower, Alojzy lunged, grabbing hold of his ankles. His left hand screamed, but he put the objections in the back of his mind. Szyman. He would stop Szyman.

The large man fell forward onto the stone pathway and dropped the jar on the ground.

"No!" Szyman shouted, spitting blood from his mouth.

Alojzy pushed Szyman aside and grabbed the jar. He stared at the yellow concoction. "What's so special about this?"

"Al...please," Szyman begged. "Just give it back. Please. It's important."

"I'm guessing this jar isn't marmalade." Alojzy twisted the top.

"Al! Don't!"

"Why? You don't want me to discover your secrets?"

"No, it's—"

Alojzy removed the lid.

Yellow smoke exploded out of the jar.

And Alojzy flew into the Keep's wall.

TWELVE

The world spun.

    Shouts bellowed.

    Yellow.

So much yellow.

And then he gasped.

With his head pounding, Alojzy stumbled up from the ground. Blood trickled down the side of his face. He squinted. A deep yellow fog shifted through the air, filling the courtyard.

"No! Teodozia! Don't go!" Malaika's voice rang.

Alojzy only saw the woman's shadow as it darted through the courtyard. He lost his footing as he tried to follow.

Szyman grabbed hold of him. "Al! Stop! You're hurt!"

Alojzy squirmed. "What in the name of Moltod was that? There was an explosion!"

"It doesn't matter, Al. Please, go lie down. I'll take care of it—"

Alojzy shoved him back with his shoulder, causing Szyman to stumble back towards the Keep. As he landed, the yellow mist dissipated, revealing the broken stones of the Keep scattered throughout the courtyard.

His home, his pride, destroyed by a sudden wave of magic. It was as if someone took hold of his heart, grabbed it in their hands, and ripped it to shreds. Every moment he spent planning this home, left to waste in the rubble.

Gone.

Forgotten.

Broken.

Everything he'd done for Moltod, destroyed by untamed magic. Perhaps what the Kainan soldiers said had been true: magic was the product of Leycie's inability to control abstract and chaos. Untethered and broken, it had nowhere to go but to destroy.

Did Moltod give Alojzy this new magic to battle Leycie's horrors?

Is that why he survived?

Alojzy approached Szyman. "You couldn't just take my wife. You couldn't just hold secrets from me. You had to destroy my pride and joy!"

"What are you talking about, Al?" Szyman raised his hands in defense. "I have taken nothing from you."

Alojzy grabbed a stone from the ground, his body shaking as he approached Szyman. "You're Celina and Elzbieta's father. You bed my wife on the regular. MY wife. I've seen the way you two laugh together."

"Al, I've never slept with Dobroslawa. She and I are friends—"

"Don't say that! I know the truth!"

"You're disoriented, Al. Let's lie down. It's only the Keep that was destroyed. Malaika and I will handle the monster—"

"You mean your untethered magic!?" Alojzy's rage continued to crawl through his body. His stomach twisted, lips twitching.

"I did not create that monster. She is a product of a greater power—"

"Leycie. It's a product of Leycie."

"I do not worship Leycie."

"Of course you do! You never come to the altar."

"Because I worship neither Moltod nor Leycie. There are other gods and beliefs than just yours." Szyman stepped forward, hands still raised. "Please, let's get you inside. I'll answer your questions about what Malaika and I know, about the monster, and about my relationship with Dobroslawa. I intended no harm to you."

"So, you admit you had relations with my wife?" Alojzy gripped the stone tighter. "Did you seduce her with your magic?"

"My magic is merely creating mirages—"

"Then you created a mirage of me!"

"No. I can only create mirages of existing buildings. I can create fake towns, but nothing is real! Al...I promise."

"I should have never let you stay in my Citadel. You destroyed it!"

"Al—"

"And my name is not Al!" He threw the stone. It raced through the air, pushing past plumes of yellow smoke and straight at Szyman's forehead.

Thud!

The rock hit Szyman square between the eyes. He stumbled backward, lowering himself to the ground. Around him, mirages of buildings emerged. For a moment, the Keep appeared to stand as a full structure. Then it vanished, replaced with the image of a small farmhouse. Each image continued to phase in and out of existence, flickering about Alojzy. He waved his hand through the images.

The smoky exterior of the building wrapped around Alojzy's hands. Rather than vanishing, this time, the image reformed, constructing a cage around Szyman. He had wanted to imprison Szyman...and Moltod had listened.

My power is growing. Thank you, Moltod.

Alojzy picked up another rock. This time, rather than throwing it, he stepped towards the cage. The cage opened for him and him alone.

Szyman raised his head as Alojzy entered. Blood covered his face. "Alojzy..."

Alojzy raised his new stone.

"You are like me... that's why you can do this..." Szyman choked.

"I am nothing like you."

"But you are."

"NO!" Alojzy slammed the rock into Szyman's face.

Once.

Twice.

Three times.

Four.

Bones cracked beneath the stone's pressure. With each hit, more blood pooled out of Szyman's mouth, eyes, nose, and ears. After one finally hit, his skull split open, leaving a pool of blood seeping at Alojzy's feet. He stared down at the man, the liar, the thief. How dare he steal everything from him! For years, Alojzy had waited patiently.

And upon dropping the stone, it was as though a new weight had lifted from his shoulders.

Alojzy breathed out, a smile trickling on his lips. He stepped out of the fading cage around Szyman. No one would question him now.

This was his Citadel. He was its master.

No one could stop him.

Not a single person—

A cold surface pricked his neck.

"Alojzy!" Dobroslawa's voice rang behind him. "How could you!?"

THIRTEEN

Dobroslawa's blade pricked the center of Alojzy's back. He turned to meet her tearful stare. She trembled, tears forming in her eyes. A few paces back, Celina and Elzbieta watched in horror, like ghosts blending in with the drab, misty surroundings.

"I apologize, my wife. I'm afraid I had to sacrifice your lover for the greater good." Alojzy hissed.

"My lover?!" Dobroslawa snapped. "I've told you time and time again that there was *nothing* between Szyman and me. He's like a brother... I've known him since I was an infant! I would never want *that* with him." Dobroslawa lowered her weapon slightly. "We may not be in love, but I have been loyal to you, Alojzy."

"I cannot believe you."

"Why? Because I was so close to Szyman!? I told you, he is like a brother to me! Nothing more! And even if I felt that way about him, it would never have happened. He has never had any sort of interest in that type of interaction with anyone!" Dobroslawa choked. "But that doesn't matter to you, does it? He's already gone."

"Your words change nothing." Alojzy laced his hands behind his back. His left hand ached. He didn't quite believe Dobroslawa, but the destruction behind him proved the dangers of a mage like Szyman. Magic, untamed and unaware of its nature, only bred chaos.

Dobroslawa kept her sword extended, gaze still locked on Alojzy. She swallowed once as if trying to hide the tears obviously gathering in her eyes. "I always admired your poise, Alojzy. I never thought you'd act this irrationally."

"Do not belittle my decision-making. Every decision I made today, I accumulated over years." Alojzy pushed her sword away from his chest. "Take the girls and go back inside. We will discuss the future of my Citadel shortly."

"This is not your Citadel. This is *our* home. And you have violated its sanctity by murdering a commander in the Evylain army outside of Moltod's altar."

"It was Moltod's will."

"Moltod does not celebrate death."

"I know what Moltod celebrates."

"You're lying to yourself."

"I know the prayers."

"No, Alojzy, you've devoted yourself to a lie and have let life escape. You have lived in a dream. You view everything through these smoke-filled glasses. For Moltod's sake, you don't even *know* your own daughters!"

"Because they are not my daughters."

"But they are. We can go in these circles for days, but they are your daughters. And even if they weren't, even if there was a semblance of doubt, they are children. You could have still welcomed them into your life, into your beliefs, but you pushed them away. You didn't even remember that today was their twelfth birthday. They chose their gods today, Alojzy."

Alojzy glanced at the twin girls standing in the far corner of the courtyard. They both wore beige robes, hands clenched, heads bent.

"Who did they choose?" Alojzy asked.

"It does not matter." Dobroslawa paced away from Alojzy. "Besides, as you claim, you are not their father. Not in spirit, not in heart; so you have no say in their god."

"Dame Goryl, I demand you tell me." Alojzy stepped forward. As he moved, a thick smoke followed him. It gathered at his feet, building like towers to his knees.

He took a quick glance over his shoulder at Szyman. The man still lay there, cold and dead.

Whack.

Pain shot through his head again, and he stumbled backward. He didn't turn as Dobroslawa lunged at him, sword unfurled. She threw him into the wall, pressing her blade to his neck. Fury scribbled its way across her face. Her daughters screamed across the courtyard. If anyone else watched from the towers, they didn't react; they didn't dare help him.

The only one who cared was the Citadel, singing its mournful song.

If only it could rise, suffocate his foes, and defend him.

In the name of Moltod, he had to live.

"I really respected you, Alojzy," Dobroslawa said as she held the sword to his neck. "But you will pay for your crimes."

"Do you intend to kill me, Dame Goryl?" Alojzy dug his fingers into the stone.

Dobroslawa stared long and hard at Alojzy. She still had lovely brown eyes. When they had first married, he stared into them, taking in their pleasure and fear. War had not hardened her gaze; motherhood had not made her weak. There was a balance in her gaze that, even now, Alojzy had to respect.

She lowered her sword. "Leave."

"What?"

"Leave. You either leave or die."

"You cannot take me from my home."

"You lost your home the moment you spilled blood here!" Dobroslawa raised her sword again, still shaking. "Please. I do not want to kill the father of my children. You may not believe they're your children... but they are. Please... leave."

Alojzy straightened his back, still keeping his fingers laced into the stones. Dobroslawa stepped back from him, placing her sword in her hilt as she walked back to her children at the other end of the courtyard. She threw her arms around both of the girls, her eyes still firm on Alojzy.

He had a choice. She had laid before him, clear as day.

Leave. Or die.

In Moltod's name, he had to choose.

But one would let him return, soon, when the time was right, to his Citadel.

He unclenched his hands from the wall. "Very well. I will leave."

Dobroslawa bowed her head but did not reply.

Alojzy did not expect her to speak. He did not expect her to follow.

Nor did he expect her children to cry.

In silence, he left the courtyard, stepping one foot at a time towards the exit of his Citadel, leaving behind a legacy crumbling at his heels.

FOURTEEN

Alojzy wandered into the Schanifeld, glancing back every few minutes at his Citadel fading into the distance. His head pounded with every step. Sleep begged for his attention, but he kept walking. He marched with pride, holding his beliefs and hatred close. It might have made more sense to vanish into the heart of Evylain, find a new town, and start a new life. But he had no one. When was the last time he even talked to his parents? Or made any friends?

No, it was best to vanish.

The Schanifeld called him. Perhaps there, he would find the true voice of Moltod.

Or at least there, he might thrive.

So he wandered, stopping at small villages scattered throughout the Schanifeld to heal his wounds, then later only for a bed, food, and water. He had no money, had no prospects, but mostly, people were kind. He traded his architectural skills for food, water, and rest, using a fake name to hide his identity. For all he knew, Dobroslawa sent word out across the plains, warning these independent villages of his presence.

In his travels, he was nothing more than a nameless architect offering his help.

All the while, his resentment grew. He had no way to reclaim his Citadel. Not without an army. Even Moltod wasn't strong enough alone.

Yet he felt Moltod's presence as he wandered through the Schanifeld. It hovered around him as a deep, thick mist. He practiced manipulating it more than he did in his private library. He refused to let the power's chaos overwhelm him. Rather, he would hold it tight. Control it. Master it.

Because Moltod mastered chaos.

So would he.

Each morning, as he wandered across the Schanifeld, he practiced with the mist. Alojzy let the mist gather around him as he walked and focused on each of its movements. It was like building a castle; he etched his fingers through the air, imagining what to build next. The mist followed his plan, one piece at a time. It was like laying bricks. Each time he moved his fingers, the mist would stack.

Perhaps he might build a new home out of nothing. After all, this magic produced more than mirages.

After traveling for weeks, hopping between independent towns, Alojzy found his way to the cliffside bordering the Blood Sea. Below the cliff, a small town waited, only a half-day walk if his calculations were correct. He was far enough from Evylain to no longer feel threatened. And with the sight of the Blood Sea, he imagined nowhere else to build his new home and pledge to Moltod.

He closed his eyes, letting Moltod's mist wrap around him. He had spent days imagining his new home. Now, he pictured it bright in his mind's eye: a simple, one-room stone home with all his living essentials and a small altar to Moltod.

Please, Moltod, I pray you will let this work. I am controlling the chaos and abstract. Please, if you have given me this magic, then let me succeed. I am nothing but your loyal subject.

He inhaled once, then opened his eyes.

A smile tore open his face.

Just as he had planned, a small room had formed around him. A bed sat in the corner, with the chamber pot hidden at the foot of the bed. A small kitchen and cackling fire sat opposite his bed.

On the wall opposite the window and the door stood the altar to Moltod.

Alojzy half laughed and pressed his hand to the wall. While it still held a strange, misty exterior, to the untrained eye, no one would expect this to be anything more than a simple home.

He'd done it! Moltod had graced him with control over this horrid magic!

Who could stop him now from creating a new life here, on the cliffside? He could rebuild.

After all, wasn't he the architect?

Building was his specialty.

FIFTEEN

Alojzy spent months building his new castle. It in no way had the prowess of his first Citadel, but it stood over the cliff, garnering whispers from the town on the seaside. The rumors spread fast; they claimed Alojzy was a messenger from their god, positioned on the hill to watch over them. They left offerings on his doorstep of food and gold, while others prayed outside his window, begging for his mercy. Alojzy passed to them the words of Moltod but never corrected their prayers.

Their belief in him allowed his magic and new castle to grow. Finally, someone gave him respect and honored his work. His parents had tossed him to the side. Dobroslawa had claimed the castle as her own... but this town worshipped him.

People from far and wide stopped at his castle; Evylain natives, Kainan soldiers, and even people from the small nation of Merton. He would hand them blessings from Moltod, and they'd leave with a prayer on their lips. More than anything, Alojzy prayed they would take his prayers and follow them, dubbing more beneath Moltod rein.

But he added his own flavor to the prayers. He never mentioned Leycie, informally banishing her from the stories and tales. Moltod was the only word he carried, like the men of Kainan carried Moltod into their hearts.

As his new home grew, he welcomed foreigners to stay, but only with the promise of prayer. With any whiff of magic, he sent them on their way, closing the door and locking it shut.

He would not have someone like Szyman knock on his door only to destroy his life's work once more.

The strangest foreigner came one night as a storm left behind a steady fog on the horizon. Alojzy answered a knock on his front door, only to be greeted by a man taller than the entranceway to his home. The man ducked his head as he entered, removing a burgundy hood and unfurling his long black hair. He rubbed his beard once, then turned to face Alojzy and spoke with a raucous tone, "Did you make this place?"

"I built this castle, yes. Are you here to pray?" Alojzy stared up at the man. His height did not scare him, but rather the way the mist followed him.

"You could say that." The man removed a flask from his side, took a sip, and squinted at another wall. "You are Alojzy Gorski, yes?"

"I am. The altar is this way if you would like to—"

"Not necessary."

"Sir, I apologize, but this is not a home for charity. I provide places to stay for disciples of Moltod."

"Yes, I know." The man pressed his finger to the wall and dragged it down the stone. "You really created this..."

"As I said—"

"Not built. Create." The man stared down at Alojzy. "Did you use the mist?"

"I..."

"It is clearly magic. Tell me."

Alojzy nodded. "Yes, I created it with magic provided by Moltod."

"Hmph. Moltod..." The man sniffed his fingers before putting them in his pocket, "Moltod... that is your god of Death, yes?"

"He is my god. Death might be part of his wisdom, but it is not the only thing he stands for in this."

"So would the better word be... Eternity?"

"Yes, that is correct."

The man circled the room, continuing to examine the architecture. Alojzy considered telling him to leave, but the man could snap him in two if he wanted. *Be patient.*

"I have known of many gods who wear the same cloak. I grew up knowing the god of Xiao Gui, but I have also heard him called Kifo Kibaya, Moltod, Morti... and Ningursu."

Alojzy laced his hands behind his back. The man had caught his attention. "You've done much traveling then."

"Yes, much." The man took another swig from his flask.

"Why do you come to my small altar, then? Surely, you've seen better castles of worship."

The man gulped, holding his finger up as he finished downing his drink, then said, "But no one constructed one with the god's own hand."

Alojzy glanced at the interior walls and furrowed his brow.

"I am not a supporter of this magic, but even I admire its beauty. It is without a doubt an ability blessed upon you by Ningursu himself."

"I thought you said your god was Xiao Gui?"

"It was. That is what I called my god when I was a child, but then I learned his true name. His true nature.

Ningursu. He is the God of Death, of Eternity, and of Abstract. He is Moltod, as you call him."

"And what makes you so confident?" Alojzy asked, eyeing the man. He considered banishing the man from his home, but the way the mist followed him kept Alojzy's curiosity afloat.

"Because I am Jiang Mǐn, Ningursu's messenger and loyal subject."

Alojzy couldn't take his eyes off the man, continuing to watch the mist rise and fall around him as if Moltod kept his fingers tight on his skin. "Do you imply you are one of Moltod's angels?"

Jiang Mǐn glanced into his flask, a smile on his thin lips as he spoke. "You could say that I am his angel. But I prefer messenger...or keeper. We have seen your loyalty and prowess over these last few years, Alojzy. I have come now to offer you more."

Alojzy didn't speak at first. Was this man making a fool of him? Moltod never dared step foot at anyone's doorstep; it was only when death came that he arrived. But Alojzy had devoted his life to his god, built not one but two Citadels, and embraced the chaotic magic Moltod had blessed him with at Szyman's death. Wouldn't it be poetic to be given Moltod's highest respect?

Wasn't that what Alojzy always wanted?

He finally spoke to Jiang Mĭn, "Prove you are an angel."

"Proof. Yes, I expected that. Fine. Follow me."

"At night? Herr Mĭn, that does not seem like the wisest idea."

"Fine. We shall venture out in the morning." The man secured his flask to his belt. "And please, I hate my given name. Please, call me by my family name. Call me Jiang."

SIXTEEN

The next morning, Alojzy followed Jiang the Giant out into the Schanifeld. Every few steps, the mist gathered around Jiang, causing him to race forward faster than Alojzy could keep up with him. The giant slowed his pace, grumbling to himself in a foreign tongue. Alojzy wasn't sure what the man was going to show him, and a soft paranoia seeped into his thoughts. What if this giant was taking him into the Schanifeld as a sacrifice? What if he was one of Dobroslawa's men? What if he was one of Leycie's angels, come to take him away?

The man showed no desire to fight. Every few minutes, he opened his flask to take a drink, but even in a half-inebriated state, he had more sense and serenity than most men. Jiang marched like a man on a mission, with a destination locked and in mind.

After walking for three hours in silence, Jiang finally stopped at the top of a small hill. Alojzy caught up to him, heaving, and followed his gaze. Bile rose in his throat upon seeing where Jiang had taken him.

Over the hill lay over thirty bodies of Kainan soldiers, beheaded and broken, with their blood staining the white flowers of the Schanifeld. Smoke rose from suffocated fires while tents lay scattered in shambles.

"A battalion from Evylain must've been here..." Alojzy murmured.

"It doesn't matter who was here. These men are dead. And now we have a job to do." Jiang took a step forward down the hill.

"A job? They are already dead. Has Moltod not already done his duty?"

"He may have, but *our* duty has only begun."

Alojzy asked no more questions as he followed Jiang into the heart of the battlefield. Already, it wreaked of the dead. Jiang seemed undeterred, kicking one of the decapitated heads to the side and stepping over bodies like fallen trees. This was not the first time Jiang strolled through the valley of the dead. That much was obvious by his nonchalance.

And as he sat down amidst the blood, he did so as if their king.

"It is time," Jiang stated as he placed a hand on the head of a bloodied young soldier.

Alojzy opened his mouth to ask a question but stopped. Jiang had fallen into a trance-like state, eyes rolling back in his head, mouth ajar. It ended in a blink as mist rose around him. Before them, the smoke transformed into a ghost of the dead soldier on the ground. It stared at its body, then dissipated into the air.

Jiang rose at once, moving on to the next body.

"What did you do?" Alojzy asked.

"I released his soul."

"Why? What purpose does that serve?"

"It is my duty, as a Mist Keeper, to deliver souls to Ningursu."

"Ah, yes. Moltod collects souls for the afterlife..." Alojzy glanced over the battlefield. "Why does he not do it himself?"

"The world is vast, and *Moltod*, as you call him, is ancient. He needs those by his side he can trust—a Council, if you will, of Mist Keepers."

"Mist Keepers... Are those what he calls his angels?"

"If that is what you want to call us, yes."

"Us...a Council... So there are many of you?"

"There are six if you include Ningursu. Each of us serves a role, with the youngest serving as the primary releaser of souls. The current releaser is aloof, though. She does not perform her duties well, but she does them as needed. In fact, she was supposed to come find you but vehemently refused, so Ningursu sent me instead." Jiang eyed Alojzy carefully. "We want to offer you a chance to be on our Council and a chance to be your Moltod's 'angel' for all eternity."

A chill ran down Alojzy's spine. Every day, since he was a mere child, he wanted to be nothing more than Moltod's loyal servant. He thought that meant building a castle, constructing a patronage, but the true servants had always been the angels.

Alojzy knew their truth. "I know well enough that to be a true subject of Moltod, it means death. As you can see, I am not dead."

"In time."

"How do you know?"

"If you train, you will succumb to a curse of death," Jiang said without flinching.

Alojzy eyed him. "And if I refuse?"

"Then your magic will certainly reach its finality, perhaps diminish. But with the way you have already harnessed the miss, I believe you would be quite successful. After all, Ningursu wants you. That should be a great honor." Jiang didn't meet Alojzy's gaze as he spoke, staring out across the field of the dead. "You don't have to decide today. That'd be ridiculous. But consider it... because if Ningursu wants you, then there's no reason you shouldn't succeed."

Alojzy said nothing. He had devoted his life to Moltod. Now Moltod wanted his loyalty. He could finally be something greater than a banished architect.

"Teach me," Alojzy ordered.

Jiang chuckled. "You are a demanding little man, aren't you?"

"I'm only asking to learn before deciding."

Jiang didn't respond. Rather, he snatched Alojzy's hand and, in a swift movement, pressed it down on the dead body lying beside him.

For a moment, all was still.

Then came the rush of black smoke.

And he fell.

Down...

    Down...

        Down...

Where he landed in a pit of darkness.

Where am I? What's happening?

Black smoke twirled. As he reached out, he felt nothing but void.

He stepped forward, but his steps took him nowhere. Alojzy had nothing.

He was nothing.

But then came a flicker of light far above him. It cast enough down to see a shadow curled on the floor in front of him, dressed in a Kainan uniform. He called out to the figure, but his voice had no sound.

I need to climb out. He eyed the pinpoint of light.

Even if he stood in a void, he knew that the mist remained. It always remained, a constant reminder of Moltod's presence.

Alojzy could control it and beckon it to climb.

One at a time, stairs appeared before him, climbing up higher and higher to the opening. The figure beside him looked up this time, then stared at Alojzy.

"Come." Alojzy's voice rang now, echoing about the void.

The figure joined his side.

And they climbed.

Up...

    Up...

        And...

Alojzy blinked. He still sat in the middle of the field with Jiang.

"Just as I thought. You already have the talent." Jiang said.

Alojzy didn't turn to face the giant.

Instead, he stared before him at the ghost forming above the body of the dead man.

It bowed to him before vanishing into Moltod's eternal embrace.

SEVENTEEN

Alojzy welcomed Jiang into his home and dove into the new world of mist that had entered his life. During the day, he traveled with Jiang to deaths within walking distance. No one noticed them as they entered homes, hidden by a cloak of mist. Per Jiang, people with enhanced sight, as he called it, could see Mist Keepers undeterred while others needed help. It proved to be a useful guise as they released souls. No one questioned why they traveled to the different gravesites or ventured into the house of a dying man. Everything benefited them, all because of Ningursu's mist.

"Soon," Jiang told them as they walked to a gravesite, "you'll be able to traverse the mist."

"Will that take me anywhere in the world? To carry out Moltod—I mean Ningursu's duty?"

"It will take you a good distance, but it is exhausting. But if you are wondering if I can go from here to the Southern Continent in seconds, the answer is no. Some souls must wait."

"That seems inefficient." Alojzy stared down at his own feet. One step, two steps, each in front of the other. Everything moved slowly. There had to be a better way.

"It is what it is and how Ningursu decrees."

"You must have at least a home. A castle, if you will."

"We have a gathering place of sorts on the Southern Continent to return to if we are tired or need help. Ningursu always resides there, but the rest of us... we find our own way."

"Certainly, that causes miscommunication."

"We manage."

"There must be a way to improve it."

Jiang shrugged and said nothing else.

During those trips, Alojzy practiced releasing souls. The void became less daunting, almost welcoming in a way. He could help each soul out with a set of stairs, a hanging ladder, or a ramp to the sky. Each soul entered the mist of Moltod without hesitation.

Well, at least the ones that deserved it.

Some souls never saw the light. They would not follow Alojzy up the stairway, remaining in their dark hell. When it first happened, Alojzy feared he did not appease Moltod, but Jiang assured him everything was well.

So, he continued, learning with each release. As more souls entered the mist, his magic grew. He composed fixtures without a mere blink, mazes with a wave of his fingers, and new rooms in his castle with a single breath. But not only did his architectural abilities grow, but other pieces of magic. He acquired different languages from the dead, increased his travel speed across the Schanifeld, and perfected his method of release with each death.

When night fell, he and Jiang talked over drinks. There, in Jiang's drunken stupor, Alojzy learned the history of the Council.

"Ningursu will be very pleased, I am sure," Jiang said one day over drinks, "I have not heard from him, but you are progressing well."

"Will I ever meet him?"

"Yes, someday."

"When?"

"Whenever your travels take you to him, or he comes to you. Be patient."

Alojzy clenched the table but maintained his composure. "I am patient. I am only inquiring."

"You always are..." Jiang poured himself a glass of wine and sniffed it.

An awkward silence always filled these parts. Alojzy would ask a question, Jiang would argue back, and then they would sit there for minutes, waiting in a stalemate for the other to speak.

Alojzy forced himself to break it. "And the others? Who are they?"

Jiang took another drink, then leaned back with his long legs propped up on the table. "Aelia was his first true follower. She's a healer, but not in the traditional sense. She heals the mist and keeps it from faltering."

"So she has magic?"

"She is a Mist Keeper, and she has abilities linked to the mist."

"Is that why I can... build with the mist?" Alojzy had suspected this for a while, but hearing Jiang say it confirmed his suspicions.

"Yes. A gift from Ningursu, I suppose." Jiang finished his glass of wine, not elaborating any further.

Alojzy didn't expect him to say anything else, so he asked, "And what of the others?"

Jiang sighed and closed his eyes. "Yes, the others."

Alojzy waited for Jiang to say more.

"There is Tomas," he said. "He uses the mist to understand people... read minds. It is quite invasive if you ask me. Next came Julietta, the poor thing. Her memory is not what it used to be, but she is a fantastic artist. She uses the mist to paint memories. Shame she can't paint her own." Jiang stopped for a moment with his eyes still shut. His body relaxed ever so slightly, bringing one finger to his long hair. He twirled it around his fingers. "Julietta trained me. And I trained—"

"You have not told me your abilities," Alojzy interjected.

"It doesn't matter."

"But it does. It helps me understand and, as you claim, succeed."

Jiang still didn't open his eyes. For a moment, he looked less like a giant and more like a man, lost and broken. But the guise fell, and he once again straightened his shoulders as he spoke, "I have no ability. Or none outside of my basic duties."

"Ningursu did not give you one?" Alojzy shifted backward in his chair.

"No, I had one. It's still there, nagging at me like a pest. But I didn't want it. I don't like magic."

"Then why be a Mist Keeper in the first place?"

"Because I saw it as an opportunity."

"For what?"

"To escape." He punctuated the statement.

Alojzy knew not to press further, but he refused to let the conversation end. He still had more to learn. He asked, "Who is the last one? You said there are six. We have talked of five."

Jiang's eyes finally opened, and he snagged the bottle of wine off the table.

As he uncorked the bottle, Jiang spoke, "Yes... the last one. I trained her, but I didn't want her to join us. She is erratic, untamed... a good Mist Keeper... but not loyal to Ningursu in the slightest. She comes and goes as she pleases. Of course, she might have the best advantage of us all. She's able to create these maps out of the mist. I don't like it. She knows where everything is; she probably knows you and I are talking right now. There is no reason for her to be missing, but she stays in the shadows and drives me mad."

"She's a cartographer of mist?"

"That's one way to put it. I call her an annoyance. She goes off hunting dragons, befriending ghosts, and searching for monsters. That is not our role... but she disregards all of that. She has been a constant headache ever since she entered our world." Jiang went to pour a glass of wine, then stopped, choosing instead to raise the bottle to his mouth and chug it.

"Is she so annoying you do not wish to mention her name?" Alojzy asked.

Jiang slammed the bottle on the table again. "Her name's Malaika."

EIGHTEEN

Malaika.

The name haunted Alojzy. Every night, he cursed her, blamed her and Szyman for his lost Citadel.

And now, her name returned, like a curse on Jiang's lips.

Malaika.

"I met her," Alojzy said. "She destroyed my first Citadel."

Jiang shook the bottle of wine, watching the liquid shake at the bottom. "Yes. We know. Because you met, it prompted your ability."

"I met her almost fifteen years ago. Why would my abilities only start in the last couple of years?"

"You did not practice. Many people with the dormant mist abilities meet Mist Keepers, but if they do not accept their powers, their powers will not grow."

Alojzy thought of the short, dark, curly-haired woman. The three times he saw her, she moved like a shadow.

Or like mist.

Even as he went to bed that night, Malaika inhabited his mind. She moved in and out of his thoughts like the mist, carrying a yellow jar of smoke and monsters. When he spied on her and Szyman, Malaika had mentioned that Alojzy was one of them.

Did that mean Szyman was supposed to be a Mist Keeper?

Did that mean Malaika knew this whole time?

They kept my future from me and wanted me to fade away into nothing.

They feared what I would do with Moltod's power by my side.

Too bad I still succeeded.

Sleep never came that night. With the moon still hanging as a mere slither in the sky, he stepped out into the brisk spring air. The waves of the blood sea thrashed against the surface of the cliff while a few lights flickered in the town by the shore.

Alojzy pulled his long coat tight around him and stared out at the Schanifeld.

All seemed peaceful, but for the single storm cloud moving across the horizon. Lightning ripped it open, and a soft growl of thunder chimed. Alojzy listened for the echoes of the dead. He'd grown used to hearing them off in the distance, begging for freedom.

While he'd never attempted to release a soul without Jiang over the last few months, the echoes called to him more than ever. It was like he stood in a tunnel, and people screamed his name. So, he followed the calls, letting the mist wrap around him, towards the direction of the storm.

Whenever he stepped into the mist, it reminded him of walking into a cave or a tunnel. It wrapped around him, pushing him towards the dead souls. It was a temporary fixture, and as soon as he stepped out, exhaustion washed over him. If he could keep these tunnels standing longer, then perhaps traveling the world would be easier. He could go not only across the Schanifeld, but across the continent, across the ocean, and to Ningursu's fortress over a single day.

He could carry out Ningursu's word with a blink of an eye.

The mist dissipated as he arrived outside another small town. Above, the storm he saw in the distance raged. This was no normal storm; he recognized its fury at once. With lightning thrashing in constant waves, with a stench of rotten eggs ripping apart the town, for a moment, Alojzy returned to that fateful day in his Citadel. The yellow smoke pulsating through this town behaved the same, coated with a layer of paranoia.

It was here.

He didn't know if it was a monster, a demon, or unkept magic... but it was here, painting the town yellow. His head spun at its presence, his heart quivered at the thunderous roars, and his eyes stung with every flash of lightning. What was this thing? Did it come from Leycie?

And why had Malaika brought it to his Citadel all those years ago?

Rather than wondering, his focus fell on the commotion as he hurried through town. If this yellow chaos had arrived, then certainly Malaika had as well.

And he could finally confront her, for they were the same, as she said long ago.

He followed the echoes, listening to where they screamed the loudest. They led him through the town, past the droves of soldiers gathering on the road, and to a gravesite. Just on the edge of town, the storm gathered with the most force. There, it took the shape of a humanoid beast with elongated arms, a half-extended jaw, and a missing eye. In facial features, without a doubt, it was human...at least at some point. But it more-so resembled hundreds of humans, stitched together along jagged seams.

Before it stood a small figure with unkempt, curly hair.

"Malaika!" Alojzy shouted over the wind.

The woman turned. She stared at Alojzy, mouth ajar, eyes wide, as still as a statue.

"So you never caught this *thing*, did you?" He approached her. "Once again, you have left it to terrorize a town, so it seems."

She snapped back into motion, "Can we do this later, Alojzy? I just about have gotten Teodozia calmed—"

"No. You will flee again without answers. But I've gotten them now. I know who I am." Alojzy stepped in front of Malaika, pulling her attention away from the monstrous storm. "I am just as powerful as you are."

Malaika met his gaze. "I know Jiang's been teaching you, but you can't believe everything he says. There's more to the world of the Mist Keepers than Ningursu's council."

"Why should I trust you?"

"Because I've seen the truth!"

"Truth of what?"

"Ningursu." Malaika hissed.

"You cannot fool me. I am Ningursu's loyal subject."

"Ningursu is not your Moltod."

"You're right. He is more." Alojzy replied.

"Have you met him?"

"Not yet. But when the time comes, I'll be ready."

Malaika chortled, "You're a buffoon. You believe whatever you hear and spew things like a book. That's why I didn't offer you an apprenticeship. I wanted Szyman to follow in my steps, but he chose not to be a Mist Keeper."

"Well, Szyman is gone. He was a pathetic man, and he destroyed my Citadel."

"*You* destroyed your Citadel, Alojzy. We had Teodozia under control, and now, for the past five years, I've been chasing after her! She's scared—look at her!" Malaika motioned to the monster.

It bellowed with a roar of thunder.

"I see nothing but a nightmare that needs to be destroyed." Alojzy spat. This monster did not deserve a name. It did not belong anywhere but the void.

"She cannot be destroyed!"

"Everything can be destroyed, just as it can be built."

"Well, she can't! Ningursu made her indestructible for a reason!"

Alojzy stopped. "Ningursu made her?"

"As I said, not is all as it seems."

"Then tell me."

"We don't have the ti—"

A thunderous scream cut Malaika's statement short. She turned back to the monster and lunged toward it. Alojzy shouted after her, but she did not respond. Her small body hurled itself into the monster's embrace, and they spiraled up...

Up...

　　Up...

Into the sky, past the clouds. The thunder grew softer as they disappeared.

But the destruction in the gravesite remained. The monster had pulled bodies from their shallow graves while stones lay toppled along the fence. Alojzy raced to the edge of the site, but Malaika and her monster had long disappeared.

No wonder Jiang calls her useless. She left these bodies behind in the void.

He considered chasing after her, but duty called. Instead, he knelt beside a body on the ground and pressed and hand to its head.

At once, the void surrounded him, and he constructed a staircase.

NINETEEN

"Halt!"

As Alojzy climbed out of the void with a ghost on his heels, he no longer found himself alone at the gravesite.

A battalion of soldiers bearing the Kainan uniform surrounded him.

Alojzy rose, lacing his hands behind his back as he met their gaze. He hadn't heard them approach, but with the bellowing winds, everything else faded into the background. *Don't fret. Control the situation.* He bowed to the soldiers. "Ah. Hello, gentlemen."

"Monster!" the Kainan Kapitän barked.

"Why would you say that?"

"We saw the storm."

"Oh, no! You are incorrect. There was a monster, but I tried to stop it in the name of Moltod—"

The Kainan Kapitän stepped forward, sword extended, eyes dark and filled with rage. He declared, "You're feeding off the dead."

"No, I implore you, Herr, I am only here as a servant of Moltod."

"So, you are a priest?"

"No... I'm one of Moltod's Angels. I am here to help the dead." He tried to speak with the same confidence as Jiang. He bore the aura. Certainly, Alojzy did as well.

The Kainan Kapitän furrowed his brow. Everything remained still for a moment.

Then the Kapitän laughed. "This little man thinks he's an angel!"

The rest of the soldiers joined in the laughter.

Alojzy retreated slightly. Of all people, he expected the men of Kainan to believe him. They looked to Moltod with more loyalty than he did; he based his entire life on their worship. But these soldiers bellowed and mocked him. When their deaths came, he might not be so kind if they behaved like this.

Ningursu would not desire disobedience in the mist.

The Kapitän approached Alojzy and grabbed him around the neck. He towered over Alojzy, and beside him, Alojzy shrank like a child. Sure, Jiang might have been a giant, but ultimately, he was loyal; this Kapitän could crush Alojzy in a minute if he wanted.

"If you are truly an Angel of Moltod, then that must mean you're already dead." The Kapitän hissed.

"Well—" Alojzy protested.

The Kapitän tightened his grip around Alojzy's neck.

Crack.

It happened so fast, Alojzy couldn't stop it. One minute, he was breathing, and the next, choking as his neck snapped in two.

His breaths stopped short. Choking, he collapsed to the ground. Pain clamored from the side of his neck and up into his jaw, past his eyes, and into his head. Alojzy lost feeling in his hands and feet while around him, the world grew faint.

As he fell into the void, the men's laughter sang a song of death.

Alojzy did nothing but welcome it.

TWENTY

Nothing.
It was nothingness.
Emptiness.
Void.
There was no light.
No breath.
No sound.
Nothing.
Alone, Alojzy wandered the nothingness.
The repetition.
The boredom.
Locked in Leycie's realm.
Trapped.
Repeating...
Repeating...

Repeating...

Nothing ever changed.

He would walk without purpose.

Without thought.

He was nothing.

No.

He was more.

Even without light, he climbed.

So, with a single wave of his hand, he beckoned the mist into the emptiness.

He saw nothing.

But he felt.

The mist weighed more than the void, and one step at a time, it transformed at his will.

One step...

    Two steps...

        Three steps...

            Four.

He followed each step towards the unknown above him. Their weight hung heavy on his toes.

One.

    Two.

        Three.

If he couldn't escape, he'd build a new world in the void, become his own savior... all in the name of Moltod.

No. Ningursu.

He had to keep climbing. Up and high.

Each step, one jump further.

Higher.

    Higher.

        And higher.

Until, at last, a slither of light sliced open the void.

It was higher than ever before, but there, twinkling like a star.

Climb.

One step.

    Two more.

        And a third.

He sensed it now, reflecting on his skin.

Just a few more steps.

And the light washed over him, breaking the pain of repetition and creating a world of unknown.

TWENTY-ONE

Alojzy shot up, gasping for air. He still lay on the gravesite, the morning light washing over him. Smoke dithered around him, finalizing his transfer from the world of the living to the world of the dead. With bodies strewn about the gravesite, he couldn't have been in the void more than a couple hours.

After hoisting himself off the ground, Alojzy paced the gravesite, getting his bearings. Everything felt the same, but the mist moved with more vigor. When he knelt to release a soul, the process occurred with no bumps. One second, a dead body. The next? A soul, entering the mist of the dead.

He stared at his hands as he released the last soul in the gravesite. Smoke pulsated from them.

Finally, he was a mist keeper.

Even if his death came by an unexpected hand.

He left the gravesite, letting the mist travel around him as the echoes of screams called him forward; this was now his role in the world. Alojzy now had eternity on his fingertips, so he would obey its command.

All day, he traversed across the Schanifeld, derailed by different souls calling his name, with the goal of reaching his castle again. For now, that would stay his home. Though, as he wandered, so did his thoughts. There had to be a way to make a castle for all the Mist Keepers and a place to worship Ningursu.

But he had to meet Ningursu first.

Yet, for now, he focused on traveling back home. The mist spun around him, forming the strange tunnel. He took time moving through the mist, observing how it behaved and how it pushed him forward to his destination. It failed to latch onto the world, so with him gone, the tunnels vanished after he exited.

His thoughts of construction dissipated as he returned to his castle. Jiang waited outside, drinking out of a flask as usual.

"Well, I'll be on my way." Jiang placed the flask on his hip.

"You're leaving? I only just got back."

"I was waiting to see the outcome of your private excursion. It's clear you do not need me anymore."

"But I have much to learn," Alojzy objected. "I know how to release souls, but there must be more."

"You wander and release souls. That is your job."

"But I have yet to meet Ningursu!" Alojzy squeezed his hand together.

"He will call you when it is time. Until then, I shall depart." Jiang sniffed his flask. "I am out of liquor."

"But where do I start?"

"You start here and then continue. That is your role of a Mist Keeper."

"I think there is more—"

Jiang turned to the mist. He brushed back his long hair, and with a breath of smoke, he vanished, leaving Alojzy standing at the edge of the Schanifeld as the next Mist Keeper.

TWENTY-TWO

Alojzy's new role took him across the world. He traversed from continent to continent, exploring new sites and releasing thousands of souls. He ventured to Kainan and admired their fortresses, towering over vagrant cities and producing the finest warriors. From there, he headed east to Heims to admire the glaciers and free their dead from the ice. The mist took him across the sea to Spinoza, where dragons breathed mist, and south to the land of Yilk, where giants once rocked the Earth. The hardest part was venturing across the sea to the embattled land of Gonvernnes, hopping between islands in search of the dead. Only then did he arrive in the mist-shrouded nation of Rosada, decorated with towers and fighting the plague of magic.

Despite the adventures that took him around the world, the job itself became nothing more than a routine. For days on end, he wandered in silence, conducting his duty to release souls. Sometimes, ghosts would babble alongside him before disappearing into the mist. He didn't mind the silence, but the routine scratched at his psyche.

And with no communication from any other Mist Keepers, he grew frustrated.

At night, he composed temporary homes out of the mist, latching onto nearby trees and caves to keep them standing. While building each home, he cursed to himself, hoping Jiang or Malaika or the mysterious Ningursu might appear before him. In all his travels, he had yet to find any of them. The world was far more massive than he imagined.

He continued to ponder how to increase his travel speed. Could the tunnels remain standing?

How?

He observed every part of nature and analyzed every element of construction. In the forests, he studied how the roots of trees bent together. In the desert, he noted how empty riverbeds and caves met. Could he use these tools to his advantage?

Could he not just build like the Earth itself?

One day, alone in the mountainous eastern region of Rosada, he took a chance. After releasing the souls of three mages left for dead, he ventured deep into the forest. The trees here towered, untouched by the human plague, their roots arching like cavernous homes. Alojzy entered one, observing the roots as they curved upwards. Slowly, the mist gathered around him, and he commanded it to latch onto the tree.

It obeyed.

Then he pushed forward, letting the mist twirl, forming a tunnel that mimicked the roots of the tree. It pushed through the ground. Alojzy followed it further and further. He had no clue how long the tunnel of mist might continue, but he did not fret. He imagined arriving on the coastline, far from the oak tree. On his own, he would have to stop three times to arrive there.

If he kept the tunnel open long enough, he might make it in one voyage.

As he pictured the beach, light crept through from an exit on the far end. He hurried along, welcoming the breath of salt water as it entered his tunnel.

He grinned upon exiting the mouth of a cave.

As he hoped, he now stood on the edge of the sea, with saltwater brimming around him. Alojzy would have run down to the water to celebrate, but his attention went back to his tunnel.

From within the cave, the tunnel remained, whistling with mist and death. Alojzy swallowed a laugh. Now was no time to celebrate. He had to ensure it worked.

He stepped back into the tunnel and followed along the same path, murmuring a prayer that it behaved as he intended.

Within moments, he arrived back in the mountainous forest.

He let the laugh escape his lips. *It worked. I gave it a foundation, and now it remains.*

Alojzy tested the tunnel multiple times over the course of the evening. The tunnel never faded; the path remained firm and alive, pulsing with smoke. Here, on the mountainside and on the shore, he'd created his next project.

Moltod, once again, might rule the world with a single blink.

And everyone would say *his* name like a prayer.

Ningursu.

TWENTY-THREE

Alojzy spent years building his tunnel system. He used the tree in the mountainous region of Rosada as his starting point, then expanded outwards, linking paths across the continent, across the sea, and across the world. Within minutes, he could travel from Evylain to Kainan. He could reach the north and south poles in twice the time. With only a few steps, he changed continents. The world itself belonged to him now, and he manipulated its connections at will. If one tunnel misbehaved, he snapped his fingers, and it would collapse. When another proved to be inefficient, he rerouted it to save time. Bound to the trees, the caves, and the Earth itself, the mist never faded.

He could see the world in a blink of an eye.

But, even with Alojzy's success, Ningursu never called for him. Nor did Alojzy find him.

Despite his best efforts to search, he had not a clue what form Ningursu would take. In his prayer books, priests sketched the image of Moltod as a headless man sitting on a throne. That seemed preposterous to Alojzy, but that image guided him. A headless man couldn't hide forever.

His curiosity often loitered over the other three Mist Keepers as well: Aelia, Tomas, and Julietta. What were their roles now? Were they watching from afar? Was anyone?

This is why we need a fortress...so Ningursu can keep his Mist Keepers together, joined as one, their powers united. Alojzy pondered as he wandered back to his castle by the Schanifeld for the first time in months. He exited the tunnel just beneath the cliff, then strode up the path towards his home. No one spotted him, as he liked it; he purposely kept his cloak of mist on, not daring to interact with the living. A select few with enhanced sight might have seen him, but mostly, he was nothing more than a shadow loitering through the world.

With his death, he placed another cloak of mist over his castle. No one else occupied it, and many whispered that it had been a product of Moltod itself.

As he approached the doors, they swung open, pouring with mist.

He froze and clenched his fists. "You."

Basking in the mist, Malaika stood in the doorway, hands on her hips. "About time you came home."

"You are not in charge of me," Alojzy snarled.

"You're right. I'm not. But I am still disgusted by everything you have done."

"What are you talking about?"

"Those tunnels of yours are completely interfering with the way the world works. The Earth will not be happy."

"I am only using the magic that Ningursu gave me to make our jobs more efficient."

"You are messing with the balance of the world! It is not what the Mist Keepers stand for!"

"How would I know the Council's beliefs? No one has spoken to me for years!"

"That's how it has always been."

"Perhaps it is time to change, in the name of—"

Malaika threw her hands in the air. "Oh, stop with your dang prayers!"

Alojzy tightened his fists. This woman, this ridiculous woman, thought she had *control* over him. How dare she! He had accomplished more in his short tenure than she had in hundreds of years. If Ningursu watched, then he had to see this to be true.

Alojzy leaned forward, his voice low, like a snake moving through the grass, "If what I have done goes against the Council of Mist Keepers, wouldn't Ningursu have summoned me by now? Wouldn't he want to stop me?"

Malaika's posture fell, and she stared at the ground. "That is actually why I am here."

Alojzy stared. "Elaborate."

"Ningursu wants to meet you. That is why I am here."

"Oh!" The tension in Alojzy's throat traveled to his stomach. A mixture of excitement and trepidation swirled in his abdomen, but he refused to let Malaika see his emotions. He kept everything level, everything calm. "Wonderful. Where is he? We can take my tunn—"

"Absolutely not!" Malaika objected. "We'll travel the mist the old-fashioned way."

"Come now...that is inefficient—"

"No. We do this my way. If you want to meet our *wonderful* ruler, then you will do this my way. Understood?" Malaika poked Alojzy in the chest.

Alojzy fumed. But if he wanted to meet Ningursu, he had to do as Malaika said.

It was what he had been waiting for his entire life.

"Very well." He hissed.

So it must be.

TWENTY-FOUR

Alojzy hated the tedious nature of traveling without his tunnels. He tried twice to get Malaika to use them, but she refused. It took them over two days to travel from the Schanifeld to a swamp-riddled region on the southern continent. He and Malaika rarely talked during their voyage, taking breaks to release souls, eat, and rest. A few times, he glimpsed Malaika as she summoned a map from the mist. She skimmed over it, checked her directions, then waved it away from her before Alojzy absorbed its contents.

As they trudged deep into the heart of the swamp, she finally spoke to him. "I apologize. I got us lost at one point. Navigation isn't my strong suit."

"Isn't your ability centered on cartography?" Alojzy asked.

"Doesn't mean I have a sense of direction about me." Malaika stepped over a root. "I think the mist gave me my magic as a joke if you wanna know the truth."

Alojzy scoffed but didn't inquire any further.

They walked in silence a few moments longer as the trees grew dense. Water flooded Alojzy's shoes, sloshing against his toes and ankles. He squirmed as it splashed up to his leg but hid his disgust with a mask of callousness.

If Ningursu lived in this swamp, then he couldn't show any disrespect.

Malaika slowed as they approached a tremendous cypress tree with knotted roots that rose from the ground like knees. It was larger than any tree Alojzy had ever seen. From its bark, red sap fell, filling the murky water like a pool of blood.

Yet, despite the beautiful nature of the tree, a different sight caused Alojzy's stomach to drop.

Chained to the trees like attack dogs, monsters lurched with misshapen bodies. Patchwork body parts hung from them, with silver eyes darting like empty moonbeams. Yellow pulsed from the orifices on their skin. While these monsters were not as big as the one he'd seen with Malaika, they still maintained the same nightmarish aura.

Malaika glanced at them once, then looked at her feet.

One monster screamed as they walked past, while another wailed in pain. Alojzy knew better than to look, and he soon joined Malaika in her downward gaze.

Their mere presence riddled his head with nightmares. For a second, he fell into the void, unable to change, unable to create. With a single gasp, he escaped, but the monsters remained, calling for him and promising dreams in place of his nightmares.

The liars.

He instead focused on the potential fortress on the other side of the tree. Surely Ningursu lived in a castle—one that overshadowed his creations. What might he learn from this grand creation? It had to be beyond his wildest dreams.

His imagination came to an unexpected halt as they rounded the tree. There, he found only a wooden shack that belonged to a vagrant.

"I thought you were taking me to see Ningursu!?" He spat at Malaika.

"I am." Malaika knocked on the door without looking back at him.

"Enter." A voice boomed.

The hair on the back of Alojzy's neck rose. The voice rang like thunder but ruled like the wind. It begged for obedience. It crawled inside him the moment it spoke, riding on the mist and latching onto his heart.

He pushed past Malaika and entered the shack.

His knees buckled.

His head fell.

His heart rang in his ears.

Ningursu.

Perched on a pillow, in the arms of a ghost, sat nothing more than a head. Half its face sat as only bone, while the other half remained coated in peeling skin. It had a single white eye that scanned the room. Mist and smoke poured from hits mouth and eye socket, dancing around the room like a prayer.

Beside the skull stood four other people. On his left stood Jiang and another man with a scar on his face. To the right of the skull stood a woman with long blonde hair and a paint-stained dress. Beside her waited a hawkish woman with eyes as dark as her hair.

"Alojzy." The skull boomed at last.

Alojzy kept his head bowed. "Ningursu, sire, it is an honor."

Ningursu continued. His voice almost sounded warm, welcoming, despite the powerful nature on his lips. "I apologize. It has taken us this long to meet. The past few years have been difficult for our little family.

But I am happy to meet at last. Please, rise. I would like to see you eye-to-eye."

Alojzy obeyed, clenching his hands together as he climbed to his feet. He glanced once over his shoulder quickly, but Malaika never followed him into the room.

"Let us formally welcome you to our little Council," Ningursu said. "I know you have already met Malaika and Jiang, but let me introduce the others to you."

Alojzy once again turned his attention to Ningursu. "Of course, sire."

Ningursu turned his attention to the other Mist Keepers. "I'd like to introduce you to Tomas."

The man with the scarred face bowed his head.

"Aelia."

The woman with dark hair bowed.

"And Julietta."

The woman with the paint-stained apron waved slightly, her eyes distant and unfocused.

"This is our Council of Mist Keepers. We are so happy you are to join our ranks." Ningursu produced something that looked like a smile, but it was hard to tell with only half of his lips on his head.

"It is an honor, sire," Alojzy whispered.

"We've been watching you since before and after you joined the mist. Your abilities have solidified in an intriguing way."

"Thank you, sire."

"Now I have a couple of questions for you."

Alojzy licked his bottom lip. Was this what Malaika had been inferring back in his castle? Was Ningursu going to scold him and take away his powers? Alojzy couldn't refrain from saying, "Sire, everything I have done has been for you."

Ningursu chuckled, "Of course, Alojzy. I would not expect it otherwise. I only want to gather a more well-rounded understanding of your magic, that is all."

Alojzy relaxed.

Ningursu waited a moment, then continued, "Now tell me, is it true that you can build with the mist?"

"Yes, sire," Alojzy answered at once.

"And you have been building a tunnel system?"

"Yes." Alojzy did not question how Ningursu knew. He was a god, after all. Of course, he knew.

"Fascinating." Ningursu closed his white eye, "Very fascinating. I would love to see it."

Alojzy maintained his composure as excitement simmered through his chest, "I am happy to show it to you anytime, sire."

"Could you show it to me now?"

"If that is what you desire."

"Excellent." Ningursu glanced up at his ghostly companion. "Nedo, hand me to Alojzy."

The ghost placed Ningursu in Alojzy's hands, then stepped back against the wall. Alojzy balanced the skull carefully. It was strange; he held the literal God of the Mist in his hands. One wrong move, and he could vanish.

"Do not fret, Alojzy. All is well." Ningursu said, then turned to the others, "You are all dismissed. I wish to work with Alojzy in private."

The Mist Keepers bowed their heads in unison, then filed out of the hut. Alojzy waited a moment and, as if a Kapitän bellowed a command, began his march back into the swamp. He kept his tense confidence, taking care with each step into the mud.

Alojzy took Ningursu to an arched hole in the side of the cypress tree. He ducked under its bark and let the mist wash over him. One step at a time, a new tunnel formed, connecting to his endless network. The tunnel clung to the walls of the tree, using the dripping red bark as its foundation. As it formed, it widened, opening at a junction where hundreds of tunnels came together.

"Fascinating," Ningursu said as Alojzy slowed to a stop. They stood there in silence, listening to the tunnels howl.

Alojzy could only fathom what went through this ancient skull's mind: amazement, fear, disgust? He hadn't a clue where his thoughts might land.

"Can only you access these tunnels?" Ningursu asked.

"Oh," Alojzy pondered for a moment, "I imagine any of the Mist Keepers can access them. I have not shown these to anyone else yet."

"What about the living?"

"The tunnels are shrouded in mist and earth. I can't imagine any living person being able to access them. At least not on their own." He scowled to himself. But what if someone, granted with Leycie's magic, could enter? Surely Moltod—or Ningursu—might be strong enough to fend off such an intruder.

"Good...good..." Ningursu produced that strange smile again. "I want you to understand, Alojzy, our Council is under constant threat. I have been searching for ways to protect us for many years, and it ultimately led to every member scattering."

"That must be inefficient."

"It is, but it has been the only way to keep our power in line. There are many foes...many monsters..."

"Monsters." Alojzy recited.

"You saw those monsters by the tree, yes?" Ningursu asked.

"I did." Alojzy trembled as he envisioned the creatures lurching and throwing themselves into the trees.

"They are just one of many things threatening our Council. Each threat wants to see us end, to abolish this Council and create a new imbalance in the world. But we, as the protectors and guardians of Death, must stay strong." Ningursu paused, letting the brevity sit in the air. Alojzy inhaled it, his own fears bleeding. As he expected, the monsters were born of Leycie's dominating hand; if left to roam, then Leycie would dominate, and Moltod would fall.

Ningursu continued, "Do you think, Alojzy, that you can build us a place where we will be safe from these monsters and where we can imprison them for eternity? Perhaps even a place that we could call... dare I say it... home?"

Alojzy glanced down at the tunnels. He had already built a Citadel and a castle in the name of Moltod. This was what he had been waiting for since Jiang told him of his fate.

"Tell me what you want, sire. I am at your disposal."

TWENTY-FIVE

Each day, after conducting his releases, Alojzy returned to the swamp to confer with Ningursu. His request seemed simple enough: a secure location for the Council to thrive. It was something they hadn't had for hundreds of years. After altercations with many opposing forces, safety became nothing more than a dream. Ningursu turned the earth into their home, hiding relics around the globe and scattering his secrets into the mist. When Malaika joined the Council, for a moment, Ningursu told Alojzy that he believed they found solace. She could keep track of everything with her map. But with her elusive and chaotic behavior, she proved to be more of a nuisance than anything.

Alojzy could take that control from her. Soon he would know the world.

To set up his new masterpiece, Alojzy used the swamp as his base. The giant cypress tree beckoned to him, bleeding with stories of the past on its bloody skin. He entered through the gap in the tree. Rather than following down the tunnel he created, he ordered the mist to hollow out the ground beneath the tree, using the trunk and roots as continuous walls.

Around him, the mist spun, filling the new hole. He would work out the finer details later to transform the newfound facility into something of grandeur.

The first goal was direct and simple: to build a crypt to hide the monsters away, deep beneath the earth. With a gated lattice hidden in the back of the fortress, only those who dared dance with nightmares might consider entering. The prison itself did not hold the same stability as the rest of the fortress. Rather than clinging to one design, Alojzy spent hours turning the crypt into a maze. He let the mist shift in and out of existence, and the cells twist and turn. What better way to confuse a monster than let it struggle in a maze?

For Alojzy, a maze meant abstract and uncertainty, the exact beliefs he held dear.

For these monsters, these products of Leycie, these mazes would represent their fear.

With the crypt completed, Alojzy unchained one of the weaker monsters from the cypress tree. It stared at him with empty silver eyes and followed without a fight. It produced guttural noises with each step.

As they entered the entrance to the cypress tree, it slowed, turning its face back to the light of day.

"Come." Alojzy ordered.

The monster wheezed.

"Now!"

He tugged the chains, and the monster stumbled in behind him. It continued to grunt and moan as Alojzy led across the empty floor of the fortress. When they reached the crypt's gate, the creature tugged on the chains.

"Pluh... pluh... pluh..." the monster begged.

"Come." Alojzy pulled again on the chains.

The monster tugged back every step of the way, but despite its horrendous appearance, it had not enough strength to fight.

Alojzy pushed it into a cell deep within the crypt, and with a wave of his fingers, the door locked. The monster threw itself into the bars once, causing Alojzy to jump away from the door, but it gave up after that one failure, slumping back to its corner. Alojzy then snapped his fingers, and around him, the crypts twisted. The monster traveled with the moving cell, screeching as the maze thickened.

It spun and danced, the world under his control. Alojzy stood in the center of it all, like the eye of a hurricane, the calm within the storm. The monster's screams traveled like the howls of the wind, but Alojzy did not flinch.

He controlled it all.

He mastered the storm.

When the twisting finally stopped, the monster still sat in its cell before Alojzy, head in its hands, body shaking.

"This is your home now." Alojzy hissed, then turned from the monster and ventured back to the swamp.

Alojzy spent weeks securing the crypt, placing each monster in its own cell and expanding the maze. Except for their screams, they said nothing. They did nothing.

If they ever had an ounce of humanity, Leycie ripped it away with her destructive command.

Yet, his curiosity didn't cease. Whenever he asked for details on the monsters, Ningursu gave only vague answers.

"They are the remaining monsters from when the mist was rogue." Ningursu would say.

Or "They are products of nightmares, experiments gone wrong."

As well as "People have tried to taint the mist for centuries. We have to protect it."

And the most detailed of them all: "Magic has been around for centuries, yielding powerful monsters, determined to impact the balance."

Alojzy knew better than to question Ningursu. When the god was ready to speak, he would speak.

Even if it took hundreds of years.

So Alojzy buried himself in the fortress's construction. This fortress had to be grander than all the others. This could not be his Citadel or his small castle; this was the true home of Moltod, after all. He took every question back to Ningursu, no matter how petty: what colors do you want, what do you enjoy, what do you value?

Some days, Ningursu would humor him with full answers.

"I have countless books scattered across the world. A library would be a good homage to our Council, would you say?"

Another time, he said, "I think my place shall be on the top floor, so I may look down upon the rest and know the going about of my Council."

But with details about colors and design, Ningursu replied with a chuckle, "I have lived in a shack in this swamp for three centuries now. Do what you think is right."

Alojzy spent days wandering through different cities, observing their architecture. He gawked at the archways in the giant cities in Yilk, he noted the pearl towers in Rosada, and admired the glass cities of Gonvernnes. Each one, he implemented into his new fortress.

No. His new Library.

This was no castle. This was a monument to knowledge and Ningursu.

And it would shine.

His work continued. He built three levels within the hollowed-out tree, filled with empty bookshelves. Glass walkways cast iridescent colors over the ground floor. Stairs formed an even line leading up to the second floor and the third, where the grand doors of Ningursu's office waited. He carved out separate suites and offices, building expansive lavatories with a tunnel that led to a hot spring. While this Library served as a monument, it also existed as a home.

The Mist Keepers no longer had to wander.

They would all survive here.

With word of his masterpiece, one by one, the others came.

Except for Malaika.

Each had their own requests. Aelia wished for an infirmary. Tomas asked for a fireplace in his suite. Jiang requested a galley with space to ferment his alcoholic concoctions. Then Julietta—she merely requested a door that kept the tunnels and the Library separate.

Alojzy obliged each. If this was to be their home, it had to be perfect.

Otherwise, was it really the home of the gods?

TWENTY-SIX

They did not have any celebratory festivities to mark the completion of the Library. In reality, Alojzy never expected the Library to be "complete" in the true sense of the word. As Ningursu said, the Library would forever evolve, adding more rooms, locations, and artifacts. This was the true nature of Moltod and Ningursu: evolution.

"This has been quite impressive," Ningursu said, his ghostly companion carrying him alongside Alojzy as they walked. "I have never witnessed the mist behaving so obediently to anyone. You have quite the talent, Mr. Gorski."

"Thank you, sire." Alojzy suppressed his excitement. Each compliment handed to him by Ningursu warmed him; finally, someone saw his talent.

They strode to one of the empty shelves. Ningursu had summoned ghosts to help gather books and artifacts from across the world. They moved about the Library without emotion, never arguing or complaining, reminiscent of the builders Alojzy hired all those years ago.

Alojzy picked one book from the pile on the shelf. Written in an ancient language, even with the knowledge passed to him from the mist from all his releases, he didn't understand a word.

"Soon, our treasures and secrets will this Library keep safe from harm. Which is all I ever wanted," Ningursu said. "A safe place...built by someone I trust."

"I am happy that I have provided everything you need."

"And I hope it is everything you need as well."

Alojzy glanced at the carved archways above him. The incandescent glass glistened as Aelia walked on it above while carrying a box of items. She, as well as the other Mist Keepers, carried themselves with more honor and royalty now that they had a home. No longer did they have to wander, releasing souls and finding beds; they could be secure, comfortable, and a family.

Wasn't that what Alojzy wanted long ago when he built his Citadel?

"I am content," he said.

"Then that matters the most," Ningursu replied.

He strode with Ningursu towards the stairwell, taking stock of how the Library had transformed. Even in the past day, the arrival of books made the Library feel more like a home.

Alojzy still needed to set up his own suite. He'd chosen a room on the ground floor, surrounded by books. He would build an altar in there and perhaps acquire a new drafting table. But otherwise, the Library really was *his* home; he built it in his vision, with a few helpful suggestions for Ningursu, but otherwise...it was his home.

The shattering of glass pulled him from his thoughts. On the walkway above, Aelia stood staring at Jiang. The box she'd been carrying lay on the ground, yellow-stained jars scattered at her feet.

"You buffoon!" she shouted at Jiang, "If you're going to drink, do it in your own room. You're lucky none of these jars broke!" She held up a jar.

Jiang grunted and pushed past Aelia, his flask at his side.

Aelia cursed after him before falling to her knees to pick up one of her jars. The giant did not turn.

Alojzy's eyes locked on the yellow jars. One step at a time, he hurried up the stairs, a knot forming in his stomach. He recognized those jars.

But he still inquired, "What is that?"

Aelia gathered the jars into her box. "Nothing."

"Aelia, we can trust him." Ningursu joined Alojzy's side, his ghost still in toe. "We can tell him."

"Master, are you sure it is wise? He has only been one of us for fifteen years. We didn't tell anyone else until at least one hundred, if not longer—"

"Trust me. It is fine."

Alojzy picked a jar off the floor. It was identical to the jar Malaika brought into his Citadel. "It's a monster, isn't it?"

"As you can see, he is already quite wise." Ningursu said to Aelia. He then turned to Alojzy. "This is how we contained those monsters in the crypt when they get worse. Think of them as nightmares in jars. We cannot destroy them, so we keep them close... and train them to be our allies. For if we control our nightmares, then no one can scare us, yes?"

Alojzy continued to stare at the jar. *Nightmares.* His mind transported him back to the Citadel, basking in the haze of destruction. Then he recalled the day at the gravesite, with the monster wreaking havoc above him. It bled with nightmares.

He understood its power.

"I've witnessed this monster."

"Oh?" Ningursu asked.

"It attacked my Citadel, the one I built for Moltod years ago…" Alojzy's lips grew dry. "I saw it again right before I passed into the mist. The soldiers who killed me thought I controlled it."

"Fascinating," Ningursu remarked. "Quite fascinating."

"Someone stole one from us years ago from us. Perhaps that is it?" Aelia interjected. "I am sure it has stayed in the area."

"It is a possibility."

Alojzy bit his tongue. He could tell them he saw Malaika with it; he could tell them about Szyman. But not yet. Patience, he had to have patience.

That way, he could be the hero.

He handed the jar back to Aelia, then said to Ningursu, "I will keep an eye out for this monster then."

"As I expected. Please, keep me in the know."

"Of course, sire."

Ningursu produced something that looked like a smile. Then, with a single flick of his tongue, he ordered his ghost to carry him up the stairwell and into his office, where he could watch, listen, and rule.

TWENTY-SEVEN

Alojzy left the Library with an empty jar from the galley on his belt. Without telling Ningursu, he departed to the tunnels, passing through the doors that Julietta sat carving meticulously. She smiled at him as he strode past, but he waved it off, focused instead on one destination.

He didn't quite know what compelled him to go there; Aelia mentioned the monster stayed in the area, but he'd seen it out in the Schanifeld as well. But something deep in his heart drew him home to Freiborn.

Despite having the world at his disposal, as a Mist Keeper, he had avoided the town, letting the crying souls continue to wither. Now, heading there, knots formed in his stomach; no one would see him, he'd be nothing more than mist, but this was the home that turned him away. It might have only been Dobroslawa, but no one sought after him. Even his parents, with their connections to the military, never searched for him. While the men of Kainan killed him, at least they killed him with honesty. The people of Evylain hid their deception, wrapped in the belief that Leycie and Moltod were equals.

Alojzy knew the true Moltod. Leycie could not compete.

The town had grown since he had last been there, sprawling out into the Schanifeld with an array of homes. As he walked, listening to the whispers of souls, he caught a whiff of his parents' own cries. His heart remained stone. A better man might have derailed his mission to release those souls, but Alojzy believed a few extra years in the void would do them good. Only then, when they chose Moltod, would he welcome them into his world.

Or let them stay forever.

Would it really matter if he left one soul behind in the void?

Mist twirled in the air as he continued walking, pulsing with a thick wave of nightmares. Alojzy cringed as the void swept over him. Without a doubt, the monster had to be here, waiting in the shadows for his return.

This time, he was ready.

He beckoned the mist to bend to his will, twisting like a maze with his steps. The few people out on the street paused, some holding their heads while others sat in their nausea. A child screamed. A woman cried.

All the while, Alojzy marched with the mist on his heels, eyes straight ahead at his old Citadel waiting for him.

His first fortress had changed since he left. While the two original towers stood, they had rebuilt the Keep with white marble. On its roof stood two sculptures: the headless pristine figure of Moltod with arms outstretched...reaching for the headless, flowing figure of Leycie.

Unified.

Over *his* Citadel.

The mist twisted, and Alojzy broke into a run. Whether or not the monster loitered in Freiborn, he couldn't let *it* tarnish his Citadel.

He built it in the name of Moltod.

And it would die in the name of Ningursu.

As he arrived in the courtyard of the Citadel, the walls caved in around him, locking the outside world from his old home. Alojzy commanded the mist to take hold of the Citadel. He would make sure his Citadel obeyed, just as his Library did.

It belonged to him.

He announced his presence with a storm. Around him, the stones trembled. Doors flew open, windowpanes cracked, and with a single command of his fingers, the statue of Leycie tumbled to the ground.

She shattered into pieces.

Only her hands remained, landing at Alojzy's feet.

Let her fall. This was never her home. And it never shall be. This is Moltod's altar.

And my rule.

He kicked the statue's hands to the side and took another step forward, glowering as people fled from the Keep. They might not see him, but he hoped they felt his anger sifting through the air.

Let them feel the wrath of the god they betrayed.

He would not falter.

As the final patrons exited the Keep, Alojzy froze. A hulking figure with a thick blond beard followed from the rear.

The figure's eyes locked onto his face. Mist pulsated from its hands.

"Szyman!" Alojzy shouted.

The man blinked, mouthed something, then vanished into a passing cloud of yellow smoke.

Alojzy raced forward. Already, Szyman had vanished... if he had been there in the first place. In his place, only smoke remained. He couldn't have been there, right? Alojzy saw the man fall, cold and dead. He was not a Mist Keeper. Even Malaika said that much; he had rejected Ningursu, rejected eternity.

No, it had to be a trick. A mirage.

Or a nightmare.

Nightmare.

He stepped towards the Keep. *Think of them as nightmares... locked away in jars.*

As he entered the Keep, he removed a jar from his belt and held it close. Debris lay scattered about the floor, broken glass and cracked wood. Yellow smoke pulsed around the room. It only meant one thing...

Alojzy turned to the altar.

There, as he expected, waited the monster.

TWENTY-EIGHT

Alojzy removed the lid from his jar and stepped forward to face the monster. It stared at him, mouth slack, eyes crossed. Although it appeared weaker than when he last saw it, smaller even, as if whatever nightmares fueled its existence had run thin.

It didn't move as Alojzy approached.

"Let's not make this more difficult than it has to be." Around him, Alojzy let the walls close in, tightening around the monster.

The creature opened its mouth.

Then someone spoke.

"Alojzy! Stop it!"

He glanced behind him and almost dropped the jar.

His wife stood at the entrance to the Keep. After twenty years, she'd aged like fine wine, her face worn with subtle wrinkles and her dirty blonde hair streaked with gray. She still held that sword close to her side.

But he did not fear it.

He only feared one thing: she could see him.

Dobroslawa continued, unphased by his presence, "Teodozia is protected here. She has done no wrong."

"Can you not feel the nightmares pulsating through town? It is clearly a plague on this town."

"They only started when you arrived."

"Liar. It is a monster." Alojzy stated.

"She is my friend."

"Because you are a monster, too." Alojzy narrowed his eyes at Dobroslawa.

"No, you're the monster." Another voice spoke.

He recognized it.

Malaika stepped under the archway and joined Dobroslawa's side.

"Malaika..." he snarled.

"I've removed the shield of mist around you, Alojzy. Everyone can see you now." Malaika said with confidence.

"I always knew you were a traitor." Alojzy hissed.

"Traitor? What have I done but try to help an injured creature?" Malaika walked past Alojzy towards the monster. "I found her alone, suffering, and I have only tried to help. Years ago, after your death, Dee—"she motioned to Dobroslawa"—found me trying to nurture Teodozia in the field out there. She offered us a place to stay...and everything has been fine since! Things only go wrong when YOU interfere!"

The monster moaned as Malaika finished her sentence. She placed a hand on the monster's arm.

"This monster is nothing more but a nightmare," Alojzy hissed.

"A nightmare that Ningursu created!"

"Liar." Alojzy brushed the statement away. He could not trust Malaika. After all, he had seen the world and its truth.

"It's true," Malaika argued. "He created these so-called monsters to protect the Council from the, and I quote, 'plague of magic and life.' He is not the noble god you think he is, Alojzy!"

Alojzy glowered back at the monster, hunched over and picking at its fingers. It pulsed with mist, a product of Moltod... or a product of Ningursu. The conversation he had with Ningursu and Aelia returned to him. "Then all the more reason to lock it away. So we can control it."

"Or you could leave it and let us live our lives," Dobroslawa said.

Alojzy spun to face her. "You do not get a say in what I do! YOU banished me from my home! And now you are interfering with my new life... a life you shouldn't even see!"

"Oh, because you think you're some angel of Moltod?" Dobroslawa laughed.

Alojzy flared his nostrils and clenched the jar tighter.

"Yes, Malaika and Szyman told me everything!"

"So Szyman is still alive then!" Alojzy snapped.

"He is more alive to us than you ever were! He raised your daughters!" Dobroslawa argued back.

"They were never my daughters."

"They are YOUR daughters. I've told you that. YOUR daughters, Alojzy. He walked them down the aisle for marriage. HE acted as their children's grandfather...even though he NEVER touched me romantically. You constructed this idea of what reality is, but really, you just created your own paranoia. There was a life here for you, and you tossed it away!" Dobroslawa glanced over at the monster. "Even Teodozia was more involved in their lives than you."

"*You* banished me. Remember that."

"Because you were behaving like this! Once again, you're destroying the home you built... in the name of a corrupt God that you follow because you have *nothing* else in life." Dobroslawa unfurled her sword, her hands shaking as she pointed it at Alojzy. "Malaika says you've been given life for eternity. But what will this eternity look like? What will you think of yourself in one hundred years?"

Alojzy wrapped his fingers into the mist. "I have done what I must. And I will continue doing what I must, so Moltod, as you call him still, will reign supreme."

"And what will you do when he turns you away?"

"That won't happen. I am as loyal to him as he is to me."

"Just like you said when we wed?"

Alojzy glowered. How dare she accuse him of being disloyal! He had stayed by her side, despite her relationship with Szyman! He had built her a castle!

And he could take it away.

"You are the one who has betrayed your god. Now, you will suffer." Alojzy threw a glare in Malaika's and the monster's direction. "All of you."

"Al—"

He heard nothing else. With an extension of his palms, he beckoned the stone walls around them to fall. The Keep moaned, then with a loud sigh, the stones toppled to the ground, vanishing in smoke. Alojzy did not move. A commander amongst the rubble, the ruler of his own domain.

Dobroslawa screamed. The monster roared.

And Malaika threw herself onto Alojzy's back.

He spun out of her grasp, using the mist to leap to the monster's side. It didn't fight him, but nightmares pulsed from its skin. For a moment, Alojzy saw nothing but darkness, trapped again in the redundant void.

The void did not scare him.

Nothingness would never linger as long as the mist remained.

He visualized a staircase and climbed back into reality. He would not let the monster take him.

Instead, with the wind bellowing and the walls breaking around him, he wrapped the mist around the monster, as if forming a tunnel. It twisted and churned, forcing the monster to shrink.

Smaller and smaller... down and down...

The jar vibrated in Alojzy's hands as the monster filled the container. He forced the lid onto the opening and twisted it closed. For a moment, the jar continued shaking as if attempting to leap from his hands.

But then it grew silent.

Alojzy exhaled and let the mist rest. Around him, the Citadel lay in shambles. Not only had the Keep fallen, but so had the towers, leaving nothing more than rubble and dust. Part of him mourned the loss of his first Citadel, but the sadness vanished almost as soon as it arrived. This Citadel held no more importance to him. It was only a stepping-stone to something bigger.

Something grander than even Moltod, really.

He stepped over a few rocks, pausing at the spot where a column had landed across Dobroslawa's neck like a guillotine. Blood gushed from the opening.

Her head lay a few paces away with her eyes wide open.

Alojzy glanced over his shoulder. Malaika had long vanished, and if anyone else had been in the Citadel, they surely died.

He pocketed the jar containing the monster and stomped through the rubble. He paused once by Dobroslawa's decapitated head.

"A shame we couldn't have worked things out, my wife. Have fun in the void." He raised his foot.

Then he kicked Dobroslawa's head into a nearby stone before abandoning his Citadel.

TWENTY-NINE

Alojzy placed the last jar on the shelf in the cellar. They all sat perfectly in a row, glowing in the light of a single candle. It was strange, really, that each of these jars held a monster. In the candlelight, they almost looked beautiful.

But he had seen what they could do when let out of their cage.

He blew out the candle and returned to the ladder. One wrung at a time, he hoisted himself up to the main floor of the Library.

With a snap of his finger, he guided a bookshelf over the trapdoor leading down to the cellar. Then he straightened the books on the shelves, making sure none looked out of place.

"Is it done?" Ningursu asked, guiding his ghost forward with a flick of his tongue.

"Yes. Only you and I know where the monsters reside." Alojzy tapped a thin book on the shelf about making marmalade. "Remove this book, and you'll be able to access them."

"Good," Ningursu said. "You have done well, Alojzy."

"Thank you, sire. But..." He recalled the events a few days earlier. "What of Malaika? She clearly has betrayed us."

"For now, I shall watch her, as I always do."

"And if she releases another monster?"

"We will deal with it when the time comes. If anyone found where you hid the monsters now, I would think it'd be pure foolish luck." Ningursu chuckled, "But as long as we protect the Library, I do not think that will happen."

"Of course." Alojzy glanced once more at the bookshelf. The shelf blended in seamlessly with all the other bookshelves. No one would note it. After all, it was just one of the countless mysteries hidden in the Library and one of a few that Alojzy understood.

He returned to Ningursu's side, "Sire?"

"Yes, Alojzy?"

"Malaika mentioned that you created the monster. Why?"

Ningursu's single eye grew dark. "Ah, well, that's a long story. Let's say I created it to protect us. Now, with this Library, that sort of protection won't be necessary."

"Protect us from what?"

"I shall tell you in time."

"I'd rather know sooner than later," Alojzy protested.

"Of course you would. And you will. All I ask is some patience."

Patience. As always.

"Of course," Alojzy bowed his head. "Thank you, sire."

"No, Alojzy. Thank you." Ningursu flicked his tongue again, and his ghost carried him away into the heart of the Library.

Alojzy watched Ningursu leave. Alone at last with his Library, Alojzy took in his craftsmanship. He could stare for hours at the carvings, the melted glass, and the winding paths. Every piece of work had come together, forming this masterpiece. His masterpiece.

His domain.

He built it for Moltod and Ningursu. He built it for the Mist Keepers and to hide away the beasts.

But while Ningursu might have been the God of Death and Mist, this Library did not belong to him.

The Library, the tunnels, all of it—it belonged to Alojzy.

And if he could control this domain, who was to stop him from controlling the world?

Patience.

He had to have patience.

Someday, if he waited long enough, his domain would rise.

Someday, if he played the game right, people would carve his face into stone.

And someday, just maybe, if all went well... he would become a god.

All he had to do was wait.

WANT TO SEE MORE ALOJZY?

You can find him in
THE LIFE & DEATH CYCLE

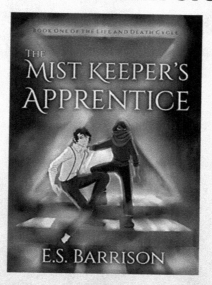

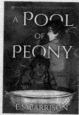

The Story Collector's Almanac

Also by E.S. Barrison...

Tales from the Effluvium
Speak Easy

The Unsought Fairytale Collection
Tuppence
Focaccia

AUTHOR'S NOTE

Thank you so much for taking the time to read *Illusions of the Mist*.

If you enjoyed this book, I would appreciate it if you could:

Review this book. Reviews are a great help to an author. If you enjoyed this book, please consider leaving a review on Amazon or Goodreads.

Tell Others. When you share this book with others on social media, you're allowing others to discover this story. Word-of-mouth is one of the best sources of marketing for an author.

Connect with me. If you want to find out about my upcoming releases, stop by my website at www.esbarrison-author.com or connect with me on social media.

Thank you!

E.S. Barrison

Acknowledgments

To all the following, my thanks, for your support, friendship, and kindness throughout this process:

First to Moira, my cover artist, for bring Alojzy to life in this beautiful cover.

To Charlie, my editor, for helping me refine Alojzy's story and show the world his mysterious past.

To Matthew, for reading the rough draft of this work, even if you only said "yeah it's good."

And finally, to my readers, I hope you have a deeper understanding of Alojzy now.

Without all of your support, this story would not have been possible.

ABOUT THE AUTHOR

E.S. Barrison has been writing and creating stories for as long as she can remember. After graduating from the University of Florida, she has spent the past few years wrangling her experiences to compose unique worlds with diverse characters. Currently, E.S. lives in Orlando, Florida with her family.

CPSIA information can be obtained
at www.ICGtesting.com
Printed in the USA
BVHW032305091122
651653BV00011B/146